I Said Yes

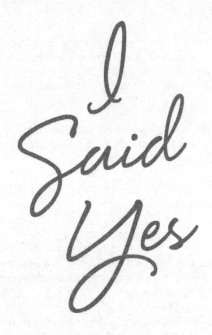

I Said Yes

MY STORY
OF HEARTBREAK,
REDEMPTION,
AND
TRUE LOVE

EMILY MAYNARD JOHNSON

WITH A.J. GREGORY

NELSON
BOOKS

An Imprint of Thomas Nelson

Published in Nashville, Tennessee, by Nelson Books, an imprint of Thomas Nelson. Nelson Books and Thomas Nelson are registered trademarks of HarperCollins Christian Publishing, Inc.

Author is represented by the literary agency of The FEDD Agency, Inc., P.O. Box 341973, Austin, Texas, 78734.

Interior designed by Mallory Perkins.

Thomas Nelson titles may be purchased in bulk for educational, business, fund-raising, or sales promotional use. For information, please e-mail SpecialMarkets@ThomasNelson.com.

Scripture quotations marked NIV are taken from the Holy Bible, New International Version®, NIV®. Copyright © 1973, 1978, 1984, 2011 by Biblica, Inc.® Used by permission of Zondervan. All rights reserved worldwide. www.zondervan.com

Scripture quotations marked MSG are taken from *The Message* by Eugene H. Peterson. © 1993, 1994, 1995, 1996, 2000. Used by permission of NavPress Publishing Group. All rights reserved.

ISBN: 978-0-7180-3844-1 (e-book)

Library of Congress Cataloging-in-Publication Data

Names: Maynard, Emily, 1986-
Title: I said yes : my story of heartbreak, redemption, and true love / Emily Maynard.
Description: Nashville : Thomas Nelson, 2016.
Identifiers: LCCN 2015013982 | ISBN 9780718038403
Subjects: LCSH: Maynard, Emily, 1986- | Converts--United States--Biography. | Bachelor (Television program) | Bachelorette (Television program)
Classification: LCC BV4935.M365 A3 2016 | DDC 277.3/083092--dc23 LC record available at http://lccn.loc.gov/2015013982

Printed in the United States of America
16 17 18 19 20 RRD 6 5 4 3 2 1

To Tyler, Ricki, and Jennings,
The three of you are my greatest gifts, and I thank
God for you every day. Thank you for showing
me what His unconditional love truly means.

Prologue

My shoulders shook violently. In between heaving sobs I tried, unsuccessfully, to sputter out something semi-coherent to one of my producers on *The Bachelorette* who had fast become a close friend. Her hand gently clasping mine, she reassured me through sympathetic nods and a lot of "Oh, Emilys" that everything was going to be okay.

I knew better.

When my gasps slowed and I could finally control what felt like an inevitable panic attack, the words finally managed to slide out.

"I did it again," I told her, sniffing as mascara ran down my cheeks, a telltale sign of the infamous ugly cry.

I was devastated. But I had to pull myself together for another round of press interviews and media appearances. I held on to the edge of the New York hotel bathroom counter-top, pots of eye shadow and lip glosses strewn messily about. Stomach churning, I whispered, this time to myself.

"I did it again."

I was devastated because I said yes to something I knew I should never have agreed to the very second the tiny three-letter word tumbled out of my mouth in front of my soon-to-be fiancé, the dedicated cameramen angling for the best shot, and, when the episode finally aired, millions of Americans. Yes to something I wasn't quite ready for.

Yes.

Three letters. One syllable. A super-short word in the English language. For many, one filled with hopes and dreams and wishes on twinkling stars. And for others, well, regret. Now don't get me wrong. I wanted to say yes to a relationship, to love, to a "we'll see what happens," you know, when the microphones turn off, the set shuts down, and the crew goes home. Just not "yes, I will marry you."

Before filming *The Bachelorette*, I was adamant to myself and to producers that I didn't want to get engaged again. I knew better. I had prematurely said yes to Brad Womack on *The Bachelor* a few short seasons earlier. I had wanted so badly to fall in love and live happily ever after that I hung on to the relationship for dear life. Hoping. Dreaming. Wishing.

Yes. I was beginning to hate that word and wondered if I'd ever get it right. I felt like a failure. Ashamed of my mistakes on and off both shows. Though I wanted to so badly, I didn't know if I could ever say yes again.

one

Church lady," my brother, Ernie, three years my senior, spewed with disgust. I pretended I didn't hear. It was a name he had called me for years. And oddly, it had nothing to do with the fact that I went to church. Because I didn't, except on that rare occasion when it didn't seem like such an enormous chore for my parents to get everyone together and out the door on time for Catholic Mass. I was dubbed the church lady because I was more or less a Goody Two-Shoes. (Maybe just one reason I had a tendency to fall for the bad boys, some of whom shall remain nameless in my vault of shame.) As a little girl, it made sense to follow the rules. I was pretty stringent. And I wasn't shy about voicing my disapproval when the ones I loved most committed certain infractions. Like smoking.

I remember when I was around ten, bouncing up the creaky wooden staircase in our home, when I heard a familiar *click-click-click* from the stove. My father was lighting a cigarette the old-fashioned way. I made a beeline down the stairs and tore into the kitchen screaming bloody murder. "Dad, don't do that!" I pleaded, tears streaming down my face. "You're going to die."

A chill from the tiled kitchen floor shivered through my body as a scene from health class a few weeks earlier replayed in my mind. The teacher had droned on and on ad nauseam about the harmful effects of smoking. I sat at my desk, barely hearing a word she was saying, riveted by a glossy photograph that was being passed around the room. There, right before my eyes, was a high-quality image of a blackened, diseased lung. I stared in horror at the charred-looking organ. So when Dad whipped out a deadly cancer stick from his back pocket, all I could think about was what was happening to his insides. Unfortunately, he didn't appreciate my good-willed theatrics. A man who stuffed his emotions, Dad simply rolled his eyes, realizing he could avoid the drama by not smoking in front of me.

Sometimes, if he was annoyed enough at my church-lady antics, he gave me more than an eye roll. Like the time we were in Key West, where we spent a few weeks most summers, and Dad reached for his crinkly pack of smokes. On cue I started ranting and raving with high-pitched cries. My father shook his head and reached for something else in his other back pocket.

"Here," he sighed, pressing a credit card into the palm of my hand. "Go on now, sweetie, go shopping."

Staying true to my obedient little self, I wiped dry my tears and nodded in compliance. "Okay, Dad. I will." It was his most expensive cigarette.

Planting roots near Cheat Lake in Morgantown, West Virginia, home to the state's largest university, my father was an old-fashioned man who held firm to some pretty antiquated values I didn't agree with but, like a good Southern girl, rarely questioned. Dad was a hard worker; he still is. Growing up with empty pockets, he toiled in the coal mines as a teenager, spending ten grueling hours per day far below the earth's surface in the presence of thick dust, heavy equipment, and noxious fumes. He worked his way up over the years and bought a handful of coal mines; today he owns two as he is beginning to retire. I loved Dad but didn't see him much as business took up most of his time.

If I was the church lady, Mom was the Southern Martha Stewart, which means, unlike the famed M. Diddy (Martha's prison name), my mother wore a lot of noisy bangles and had a slight and very charming twang in her voice. Mom poured her heart and soul into our house—cooking, cleaning, and decorating with passion. With her hair elegantly pinned up in a French twist, her feet dolled up in high heels, and the light scent of Calvin Klein's Obsession emanating from her pulse points, Mom always looked as glamorous as a 1950s Hollywood starlet. She was known for her parties. Particularly the bash she threw each Christmas Eve, where she served every delectable cocktail and hors d'oeuvre known to mankind with her signature smile. Mom was a gracious and thoughtful host. Almost everyone in town showed up to her trademark parties, teeming our old Victorian house with throngs of people drinking, laughing, and gallivanting.

My brother, Ernie, was at times protective and other times an utter goofball, knowing how to make me laugh so hard I was afraid my stomach would split.

As a relatively quiet kid and lacking even a smidgen of athletic ability, I didn't take to sports or other team activities. But I did enjoy riding horses. When I was around eight years old, I met Q-tip, a small white horse, at summer camp. I fell head over heels. My love affair with riding compelled my parents to get me lessons. As it turned out, I was pretty good.

A few years later, Dad bought me Reno, a quarter horse elegantly marked on its face with a white star. Reno was housed at a stable an hour away. He and I rendezvoused a couple of times a week, and like a happy couple we trotted through wooded trails and learned to jump with elegance over poles and cavalletti. There was just something so comforting being alone on such a gallant animal, wind blowing through our manes as the horse galloped with a beautiful combination of strength and grace. My weekends were spent out of town at horse shows with my mom and horse trainer. Some of my best childhood memories are of riding, hurtling through space and time on the back of a beautiful and powerful four-legged mass of muscle.

When I was in the sixth grade, my parents bought a farm in Bruceton Mills, which was about thirty minutes from home. The farm was smack in the middle of nowhere, in a town with a population of, like, five. Boasting panoramic mountain views, billowing cornfields, and acres and acres of fields grazed by cows and blanketed with wooded land, it was our country haven. Mom was also riding horses at the time, so Dad bought two more. As beautiful as they were, these animals were untrained. If you ever want to test your patience or will, try riding an unbroken horse. Definitely not for the faint of heart.

One weekend when I was about twelve, Mom went riding on the farm. I was near the house but could see her mount one of the horses and gallop toward the cornfields. As I diverted my attention back to whatever it was I was doing, a cry pierced the air. I couldn't tell if it was human or animal. Startled, I looked up over the field and at the same time saw the baseball hat my mother was wearing shoot high into the air. My heart started racing, and I hopped on the nearest quad, wheels spinning furiously deep in the earth. By the time I got there, Mom was writhing and whimpering in pain on the dirt. My gym teacher, who had been nearby when the accident happened, hovered over her. My dad was also there and immediately barked for me to go back to the house. There was no sign of the horse. My mom was hospitalized for a few days, and though she eventually recovered from her injuries, I was traumatized for life. I never got on a horse again.

Without riding, life quickly got lonely. I was painfully shy and wasn't talented in the making-friends department. But I did hang out with a small group of girls I had known since kindergarten. We would spend time together giggling and making up silly games at the many sleepovers I hosted at my house. We swam, canoed, and explored beautiful Cheat Lake, which bordered the back of our property. And we listened to and daydreamed of one day marrying famous boy-band musicians, my future husband being Justin Timberlake of *NSYNC. If it weren't for my mother's threats to kill me, I'd have gotten a full-sleeve tattoo of JT just so I could look at him all day long. Sigh.

The dynamic changed when I came back from spending a summer in Key West. I left the Sunshine State tanned and happy with fond memories of surf and sand. Missing my friends, I expected somewhat of a warm welcome in return. I was sorely disappointed. They turned on me. They called me names. They told lies. They started doing things and going places, making sure I knew I wasn't invited. Hurt and confused by the ice-cold reception, I withdrew inward. As hard as I tried, I couldn't figure out a reason for the drastic mutation from friends to foes. It felt pretty sucky to be blacklisted without a cause.

I know now this is typical preteen/teen behavior for girls, but hailing from a small town and being such a sensitive child, it rocked my world. I hated going to school, having to face their ridicule and taunts. I kept my emotions at bay as much as possible until the final bell rang. Then I'd run home, leaping over sidewalk cracks and stomping crunchy autumn leaves, and lie curled up on my window seat until the sun faded. The tension was so bad, my parents eventually pulled me out of school and enrolled me in a Catholic one nearby. I wasn't there long. After a short while, I found myself back at Cheat Lake Middle School. I kept as low a profile as I could, avoiding the mean girls. The further I slipped under the radar, the better off I'd be.

It was around this time my faith was sparked. While church was an occasional event, I always felt connected to God. In my heart, I knew He was real. And at times, I could even feel a divine tug, a pull toward Something, Someone greater than me. But these were feelings I couldn't articulate or put into words. I grew up believing and in some ways learning through others that God was akin to Santa Claus or a genie in a bottle. When life called for it, I prayed conditional or gimme prayers. I'm sure you know the kind. "God, if You help me pass this test / make Dad buy me that dress / tell the teacher not to call on me, I'll never be fresh to Mommy / I'll do my homework as soon as I get home from school / I'll never again forget to feed the dog" and so forth.

A weekend youth retreat deepened my ideas of spirituality. Given my lone-wolf syndrome, I'm not sure how I even ended up bouncing on a springy seat in a church van heading to a youth event with neighboring churches. But there I was. And the only thing I remember was being planted on a gymnasium floor surrounded by hundreds of bold-colored sleeping bags and their rowdy teenage owners, loud as a cavalry to the charge. I'm sure there was music, worship of some kind, a few activity-building exercises, and a spiritual message by a youth pastor or someone. I don't know what it was that stirred my heart, but something did.

We kids slept on the shiny wooden floor that night. When the lights turned out and all was quiet except for a few secretive whispers and occasional shushing by annoyed adult chaperones, I nestled in my sleeping bag, stomach side down. While cradling my head in the crook of my arms, tears fell. Silent, but many. I was keenly aware of God's presence in that moment. I didn't know Him yet, but I knew that I loved Him. The feeling was so intense, it felt as though my heart were going to explode. But for fear of being made fun of or being labeled a weirdo, I kept my head down until the tears stopped falling. I didn't share the experience with anyone. I simply enjoyed what I knew was a divine fingerprint on my life. I can't even begin to tell you how soundly I slept that night.

The summer before I entered the ninth grade, I started thinking about boarding school. My former friends still weren't being very kind, and I was desperate to start fresh, to be surrounded by kids who didn't know anything about me. At the time my brother was enrolled in an all-boys school in Pennsylvania, gracing us with his presence almost every weekend. He seemed to be doing fine, so my parents started making arrangements for me to enroll in Mercersburg Academy in Pennsylvania my freshman year.

I stared out the window during much of the two-and-a-half-hour drive. Music blared and Justin belted out the lyrics to "It's Gonna Be Me" on my CD player headset. Questions surfaced as my parents and I sailed down Route 68. What would it be like being away from home? Would I miss my parents? Would I make friends? Would anyone like me? Would I meet a boy? What if the work was too hard? Despite my fears, I felt better knowing most of the other freshmen students would share similar fears.

As we passed over the Pennsylvania border, my stomach tightened and I closed my eyes, trying to push down the ripples of anxiety that coursed through me. It was easy once we turned into the academy entrance a few winding roads later. The school was separated from the rest of the world by an ornate iron gate and surrounded by majestic trees. My mouth dropped; the backdrop was breathtaking. Mercersburg Academy was three hundred acres of sprawling grandeur. Nestled in the Tuscarora Mountain ridge, the campus swelled with manicured lawns dotted with oak and maple trees and Gothic-inspired buildings that reminded me of pictures I'd seen of European architecture. Students sporting button-down shirts, khaki pants, and bright white smiles meandered around the verdant campus, walking with enviable confidence. On the outside, the academy looked more like a country club than a school. All I could think was, *Whoooa!* I was now entering what I would quickly discover was the "Mercersburg bubble." Once inside, school becomes your world.

Orientation was a blur, as was moving what seemed like a million overstuffed boxes and bags and suitcases from my parents' car and stuffing my belongings somewhat sensibly in a cramped but new dorm room that smelled of fresh paint. After the final round of hugs, well wishes, and last-minute advice to stay away from pot, booze, and boys, my parents left. I finally had a moment by myself. I lay on my twin bed, mind spinning from information overload of classes, courses, schedules, policies, directions, and rules. I didn't know what I was in for, but based on the material I was armed with, boarding school seemed like it would be a pretty intense experience.

Boarding school was tough. I couldn't keep up academically. It was difficult to be attentive for an hour straight while professors carried on and on about things that quite frankly didn't interest me. I had trouble memorizing every fact, figure, and date from the ancient Mediterranean world. Staying focused was difficult. I was quick to zone out if something didn't immediately capture my attention. (I would be diagnosed with ADD two years later.) As hard as I tried to give my academics my all when the first semester began, I quickly lost steam. Soon enough, I was barely finishing the assigned reading and investing little work and energy into the big projects that accounted for half my grade. And without a parent, teacher, or adult to hound me into doing my homework and studying for exams, I couldn't find the motivation. So I did only the bare minimum in order simply to pass the year.

I stayed at Mercersburg for a year and then transferred to Saint Andrew's School in Boca Raton, Florida. The year before, my parents had bought a house in Sunset Key, a tiny part-residential part-resort island about five hundred yards and a short ten-minute ferry ride from Key West. They made the official move from Virginia to Florida when I started school.

While the academics at Mercersburg challenged me, the lifestyle at Saint Andrew's tripped me up. Five miles from the beach and situated in the Beverly Hills of Florida, this community, according to *Forbes*, was ranked seventh on a list of where most millionaires live. In other words, super–fancy schmancy. Though less spacious than Mercersburg at only eighty-one acres, the campus at Saint Andrew's was just as beautiful but in its own tropical way. It was an idyllic paradise. Stark-white buildings stood in contrast to swaying palm trees and beautiful tropical flowers. I am not by any means trying to take away from the beauty of the campus, but having been to Key West a million times over the years, I was well familiar with the eye-catching aesthetics of a seaside utopia. What I wasn't familiar with, however, was the blatant display of wealth.

The day we pulled into Saint Andrew's, my mom had to swerve to avoid hitting a speeding Mercedes driven by none other than a pimply faced student (who probably was just driving back from the DMV with his learner's permit hot off the press). In fact, most of my classmates drove luxury cars, like BMWs, Lexuses, and even Bentleys. They'd hop out of $100,000 vehicles sporting Gucci this and Prada that. I never felt more out of place in my life. We didn't have all that stuff up north. We had the Mountaineer Mall, home to JC Penney, Jo-Ann Fabrics, and Camelot Music. On special occasions, when my mom used to tell me I could buy whatever I wanted, I would surge through the open doors of the mall's Limited Too and leave with a huge smile, clutching a few shopping bags and a receipt for two hundred dollars' worth of clothes.

Best. Days. Ever. In Boca, if you shopped at Limited Too, you might as well be cruising garage sales.

When spring break rolled around, I went home. Sunset Key swarmed with kids also visiting from their respective boarding schools. I hung out with a few of them, and though they were a few years older, my parents allowed me to roam downtown Key West with them under one condition: I had to come home no later than 11:00 p.m. Fair enough.

We girls had a blast. We shopped in cute surf boutiques like Ego and Fast Buck Freddie's, a tropical department store where you could buy a variety of stuff, from trinkets that cost pocket change to furniture for a few hundred bucks. We loved to people watch. I remember sitting on a park bench enjoying an ice cream cone and watching the throngs of young people pass by on their way to the local clubs and bars. They were just barely twenty-one, but to me they seemed ancient, grown up, and responsible. I couldn't wait to get older!

One of our favorite pastimes was to make up stories about our identities, specifically to cute boys we met. Since the island had a heavy tourist population and we all attended schools that were hours or even states away, we figured there was no harm in lying. Chances were we'd never see these guys again. My made-up story was that I was nineteen and attended NYU, majoring in broadcasting. Granted, I'd never been to New York before. Nor did I know anything about broadcasting. But it didn't seem to matter. Most of the boys I met were interested in things other than the nitty-gritty details of my life. Lying was easy. And, I'll admit, fun. You could be anyone you wanted to be. No strings. No pressure. No problem.

One night we were waiting on the dock for the ferry. In

order for me to make it home by curfew, I had to hop on the next boat. If not, I'd be subjected to the wrath of two very angry parents. I looked at my watch. Five more minutes until the white vessel would show, bringing me home and turning me into a pumpkin. As I heard the ferry approach, I noticed we were being yelled at by a bunch of guys partying on a luxury yacht in a nearby slip. Two stories high and half a football field wide, the sleek ship flaunted elegant curves and modern design.

I ignored the catcalls. Don't get me wrong. Like any teenage girl, I loved getting attention from guys. I was just tired. It seemed as though we had been walking around downtown for hours. My feet hurt. And all I wanted was to crawl in bed, without the annoying inconvenience of getting grounded. So I just kept quiet and prayed the ferry would somehow haul in faster, as in right now. My friends, however, up for more adventure, yelled back at these guys, encouraging more hoots and hollers and eventual flirtatious invitations to board the boat. So to the tune of "Come on up here, already!" shouted by a twentysomething surfer dude with a beer in his hand, I turned my back on the incoming ferry and climbed aboard. It was the moment my life forever changed.

two

Thumping bass from hidden speakers competed with a mix of different conversations from the twentysomething guys and girls who lounged around the spacious boat. Grabbing one of my girlfriends, I yelled, perhaps a little too loudly, "Guys! My dad is going to kill me!"

She rolled her eyes, grabbed my elbow, and took me with her up a winding staircase to the top floor with the rest of the crew. The guys who had called down to us were hanging out by a bar spotted with wine glasses, beer bottles, and tumblers. My shyness taking deep root, I broke from the crowd and stood in a corner, sipping on water and enjoying the party scene away from the hubbub. From where I stood, I had a view of the glistening ocean, calm and quiet. And even with the noise, I could hear the salt water gently lapping the sides of the boat. A minute or two passed before my tranquility was cut short by a blond-haired guy with playful eyes, a strong jawline, and a sling on his arm. Good-looking with a boyish charm—this was an interruption I gladly welcomed.

He smiled and said, "Hey, you, what's up?" He was such a cutie and had a friendly and nonthreatening vibe, so talking to him felt harmless and fun. We spent the next half hour or so chatting away like old friends. Problem was, most of our exchange was based on lies, except for our names.

"I'm Emily," I said. "I'm here from NYU on spring break." I also mentioned I was studying broadcasting and was the daughter of a coal miner (true, lie, lie, and kinda true).

"I'm Ricky," he said, adding that he was twenty-one. But the best part ever was his next admission. "My dad makes seats for Ferris wheels!" (true, true, lie).

"Hmm," I said aloud, intrigued at that last bit of information. "That's different. Cool!" I didn't even know that job existed, but hey, what did I know about the amusement park industry? Ricky also told me the boat belonged to his buddy. (Lie. It was his.) I would learn later that because he came from such a prominent family, he preferred not to drop his family name. Instead, he'd often make up interesting stories about who he was and where he came from, just to throw people off. And me? Well, I just made up stuff because it was fun.

While we chatted away, I didn't think my lies were a big deal. Like any other Key West visitor I ran into while gallivanting with my friends, I imagined this night to be the last I'd ever see of him. Problem was, the more we talked, the more I liked Ricky. So when he asked if I'd meet him for breakfast at a local joint in Key West the next morning, of course I said yes.

My friends and I didn't stay long, but I didn't make my curfew. Not by a long shot. All I'll say is that Dad was not a happy camper. As I got ready the next morning, sporting a hobo vibe with my long khaki linen skirt and matching top, I looked more like a pottery shop owner than a stereotypical Floridian beach bunny. Like always, I was nervous. But butterflies weren't quivering in my belly just because I was meeting a cute boy over eggs and coffee. I felt tense thinking about our impending conversation. All cute-girl-meets-cute-boy aside, what on earth were we going to talk about? Sure we got along great, but our first encounter was essentially based on a lie about who I was, or rather wasn't. Still figuring that I'd never see him again, at least not after our date, I headed down to Camille's, a casual restaurant AOL voted "best breakfast in the United States."

Ricky was adorable, funny, and cute. And as I munched on syrup-drenched pancakes, it was truth time. My date came clean. As it turned out, his dad didn't make Ferris wheel seats. He owned a NASCAR team in Charlotte, where Ricky lived. The Hendricks also owned hundreds of car dealerships across the country. Ricky, a former NASCAR driver who had recently injured his shoulder in a race—thus the sling—owned a piece of his dad's company.

I, however, did not even think about coming clean. Ricky tried asking me questions about my personal life, but I was strategically quick to change the subject by asking the waitress for more OJ. By the time the check came, I had a little crush on the guy. On one hand, I wanted to see Ricky again or at least talk to him more because he was so cute and nice, but on the other hand lay the obvious quandary. Um, hello, people. I wasn't nineteen. I didn't go to NYU. And I wasn't majoring in broadcasting. I was, however, a fibber. Ricky and I parted ways that morning with a friendly hug and casual exchange of "see you around." He wasn't as affectionate as I'd hoped, so I figured he just wasn't that into me. Well, at least I wouldn't have to admit to lying, right?

Unbeknownst to me, while Ricky and I were having break-fast, my mom was taking a stroll near the docks and ran into the property manager of Sunset Key. He was walking with a man Mom didn't recognize but was immediately introduced to.

"Good morning, Susan," the manager greeted Mom cheer-fully. He turned to the man next to him and said, "This is Susan Maynard. Her husband, Dave, and their kids live a couple of houses down." He then introduced Rick Hendrick and told Mom that Mr. Hendrick and his wife were building a home on the island, adding, "You two are going to be neighbors!"

As the three of them talked more, my mother mentioned she had a daughter. Mr. Hendrick smiled and said, "Oh, that's right. I think she's out to breakfast with my son, Ricky."

Mom gave him a questioning look. "Really?" I had told her I was meeting someone for breakfast but didn't mention who. Besides, it's not like she was ever going to meet this random guy Ricky whose dad made Ferris wheel seats. Oh, what a tangled web we weave. As Mom and Mr. Hendrick contin-ued the conversation and bits and pieces of the truth began to unravel, Ricky's dad was shocked to discover that not only did I not go to NYU but I was also only sixteen. Yikes!

A week later, I was back at Saint Andrew's, surprisingly and giddily accepting an incoming call from Ricky Hendrick. We jumped into a great conversation that started a slow descent when he started asking questions about my classes and the fun stuff I was doing in Manhattan. Not knowing what to say, I clammed up, then blurted out, "Hold on a second, someone's calling me." Pressing mute, I hoped the pause would make him forget the questions. I don't know how exactly the call ended, but we both said good-bye shortly after I weirdly tried to dodge his questions. Again, unbeknownst to me, by that time, Ricky's father had told him the truth. I was sixteen. Still in high school. Nowhere near the Big Apple. There may have been one more phone call after that, but I was too sick to my stomach to pursue any more conversations because I had lied for so long. I was also too embarrassed to fess up. It was a lose-lose situation. I'd look like an idiot either way.

When I came home for the summer, I saw his parents around and we'd wave at each other and sometimes even engage in small talk. Years later his mom told me that soon after Ricky and I met, she had a feeling he'd end up with "Emily from Sunset Key."

In my third year of boarding school, away from the familiar trappings of home, I started coming undone. It all started in an ordinary enough way—in Jamba Juice of all places. A few friends and I hit the smoothie bar as we often did, gulping down refreshing beverages in the intense Floridian heat. By the time I had slurped most of my drink, I noticed the left side of my mouth was going numb. I couldn't suck in the last bits of the smoothie. It felt like I had just left the dentist's office after getting shot up with novocaine. I was disturbed but didn't say anything out loud. I shrugged it off, thinking the weird feeling (or lack thereof) would just go away.

That night, while tossing and turning in bed stressing about the deadline of an upcoming paper I had to write, I realized I couldn't fully close my left eye. It felt almost paralyzed, and extremely dry. I passed off the odd symptoms as an allergic reaction. Maybe there was some weird superfood or something in the smoothie that didn't agree with me. The next morning, the entire left side of my face felt slightly numb. I couldn't move part of my mouth. I couldn't lift my left eyebrow. It was as if the muscles in the left side of my face had decided to just stop working. I got spooked when I looked in the mirror. Half of my face sagged. I looked like I was having a stroke.

When I saw the doctor, he peppered me with questions and immediately ordered a blood test and an MRI. The next few days were a blur of radiology visits, doctors' appointments, and more tests. Not knowing what was wrong with me was incredibly frightening. I thought of multiple worst-case scenarios, not that I had any medical expertise to reasonably entertain any diagnosis, of course, but the fear coupled with the emotional trappings of being a teenage girl unleashed a wild imagination.

Maybe I was having a stroke. Maybe I had cancer. Maybe I had some rare disease that would soon paralyze my entire body and that doctors couldn't fix. Oh my word. How would I talk? Walk? Go to school? What if I died? What if I never got married? My heart sank at the latter.

Fortunately, some good came out of this angst-ridden waiting game. When I went for the MRI and lay in that claustrophobia-inducing coffin listening to the vacuum-like roars and obnoxious beeps, the radiologist couldn't get a clear image because my braces were interfering with the radio waves. There was only one solution—I'd have to get my braces off. Hearing the news, I did an inner happy dance. And I grinned. Well, I tried to at least. I more or less half smiled, half drooped.

I was eventually diagnosed with Bell's palsy, inflammation of the facial nerves that causes paralysis. It sounded scary, and while the doctor mentioned its cause being relatively unknown, he assured me that with corticosteroid medication, the use of an eye patch at night so I could sleep, and good old-fashioned time, I would make a full recovery. While I wasn't thrilled that my symptoms wouldn't disappear entirely for a few weeks, I was grateful it wasn't anything more serious.

When a nurse phoned my parents to tell them what was going on and mentioned the words *Bell's palsy* in the conversation, Mom and Dad rushed to Saint Andrew's. My father was unusually emotional and cradled me in his arms, whispering how much he loved me. He held me close and in hushed tones told me everything was going to be all right. It was comforting being in his strong arms. I felt like a lost little girl who had just been found. Unfortunately, the special moment was short-lived.

I sat in the doctor's office, listening to the doctor explain the medical condition in intricate detail, when all of a sudden Dad blurted out, "What?" Armed with this updated information, my father groaned loudly. His reaction indicated some sense of regret, as though he was thinking, *I came down for this?* And with that, the warm and fuzzy feelings vanished. He went back home not long after while Mom stayed behind. Her presence made me homesick. Even though she was right beside me, I missed her. And all I wanted was to go home. Right then and there.

I missed a lot of school at that point and got drastically behind in my schoolwork. I never felt I was that smart, and because of that insecurity, I wouldn't try harder or study more in order to keep up; I'd just give up. I still attended classes because if I didn't, I'd get in big trouble. Still, it was a matter of time before I was put on academic probation.

I don't know how else to describe my desperate state, but I just wanted to go home. It was the only thing I believed would make me happy. I had tried to convince my parents to take me out of school, but they refused. "We already paid your tuition, Emily. You have to stay!" they repeated over and over. I had no choice but to suck it up and stick it out.

I felt emotionally out of control. Unsure of myself. Stupid for not being able to keep up with my studies. Although I had friends, I felt alone. And suffocated by the rules I had to follow. I felt so many different things; I needed some sort of relief or reprieve from my consuming thoughts. Seeing a counselor seemed the best thing to do.

Talking to someone once a week helped some, but I was still gripped by an overwhelming desire, a desperate need to go home. My therapist prescribed a low dose of antidepressants. I don't remember them making a difference. Days passed, one blurring into the next.

I felt particularly vulnerable and sad during one session with my counselor. I sat on a white leather couch, staring out the windows of the office as a palm tree swayed hypnotically in the breeze and a turquoise sky gleamed behind. It was a beautiful day. Most days in Florida are. The sun was bright. The skies were clear. Bold hues painted the landscape from the blindingly beautiful colors of the flowers, the water, and the Mediterranean-styled homes. But even staring right into the captivating scenery, I felt nothing. Well, I felt invisible. To my parents, to my teachers, to my classmates, and even while sitting face-to-face with someone I had made an appointment to see, someone who was being paid to listen.

In that moment, the tangled mess of emotions that I nursed

under the surface started to boil. I turned my head away from the picturesque window, looked straight into the eyes of my counselor, and mumbled, "I just want to die."

Now, I didn't necessarily plan on actually killing myself. Looking back, I was probably being more dramatic than anything and figured saying something so crazy, so extreme, might warrant the attention I wanted. Or at least some kind of attention. Something was better than nothing, right? I didn't expect my counselor to take me seriously. And I certainly didn't expect the series of events that followed.

But I can see now that just like you can't yell the word *bomb* in an airport terminal without being tackled by security, you can't tell a licensed therapist you want to die and expect her to just yawn, pick her nose, and follow up with a generic, "And how does that make you feel, dear?"

My words hit the counselor like a brick in the face. Her eyes widened and she leaned in toward me, making sure she had heard correctly. "What did you say, Emily?"

The next thing I remember was being surrounded by two police officers. I know, crazy, right? I sat on the same couch, not gazing at a tropical backdrop this time but staring at two husky men in uniforms with shiny badges on their chests. They looked just as concerned as my counselor. I didn't get what all the fuss was about, especially when they began spouting an intense line of questioning.

"Miss, did you take any pills?" one of them asked, holding a pad and pen in his left hand.

"Um, no, sir."

"Did you try to kill yourself, miss?" the other questioned.

"Uh, no, sir."

The officers exchanged perplexed glances. A long pause followed. I guess there wasn't protocol for someone who said something about wanting to die but was not showing any signs of serious consideration. They didn't know what to do with me. And then, another blur. Fast-forward about an hour later, and I was being admitted to a local hospital. I sat in a waiting area wondering what the heck was going on when my therapist started talking to me about something called the Baker Act. In a calm voice and a long, drawn-out tone, to make sure I understood what she was saying, she explained how under this particular state legislation, a counselor can commit a patient to a hospital for up to seventy-two hours if she thinks that person is a danger to herself or others. As she talked, someone in light-colored scrubs walked over to me and started removing the shoelaces on my tennis shoes.

Obviously, I knew this had to do with what I said in the counselor's office, but c'mon now. Was all this drama really necessary? The mood was so tense, so serious. The nurses and aides and everyone else who rushed around me seemed pretty confident something was wrong with me. At one point, the chaos made me wonder if I really was crazy.

Another counselor came by at this point, introducing himself as the doctor who'd be examining me for the next three days to determine whether or not I was intent on harming myself. As the words tumbled out of his mouth, I could hardly make sense of what he was saying. I was so confused and kept zoning out every few seconds. So while a stranger in scrubs took my shoelaces, a doctor pelted me with never-ending questions, and a nurse started rummaging through my bag for, I guessed, guns, drugs, or needles, maybe a poem, drawing, or diary showing proof of self-harming tendencies, I succumbed to a state of mind-numbing disbelief. *This can't be happening,* I thought. *I'm not crazy. This is crazy! I'm just a spoiled kid who needs some attention.* I was petrified. Tears were seconds away from slipping down my cheeks.

What on earth have I done?

After what I assume was the process of checking in, I was given a hospital robe to wear and a small bag of toiletries that included a bar of soap, a comb, a toothbrush, and a tube of toothpaste. I clutched my swag bag to my chest, feeling like someone had taken me hostage in the twilight zone.

It was near midnight by the time an orderly helped situate me in my room, sparse and cold, where I'd stay for the next three days. An odd and nauseating smell of antiseptic and mildew permeated the air. It was so bad I could actually taste it. My roommate was asleep so I tried to be as quiet as possible, hauling myself ever so slowly onto a mattress that crinkled like plastic.

Sleep was hard to come by. The door to the room was halfway closed, but a bolt of bright light streamed in from the nearby nurses' station. Though the mild chatter and the rustling of papers from the hall wasn't obnoxiously loud, I was in such a state of shock that all my senses were magnified and the slightest sound made my skin crawl. Tears fell quickly as I thought again—and had no answer for—*What have I done?*

By the time exhaustion set in and I finally dozed off, my roommate let out a bloodcurdling scream. I jumped out of bed and ran over to her. "Are you okay? Do you need something?" I asked, panting.

My petite, blonde roommate, who was around my age,

shook her head. She looked spent. Tired, but not from lack of sleep. From life. We talked for a few minutes, and she told me she was withdrawing from cocaine. I nodded, quiet, not having a clue what to say. I felt bad for her and I could see the pain in her face, but what did I know about drug addiction? Anything I could even think to say sounded plain stupid. Like, "Sorry!" or, "Hope it works out!" I just held her hand for a bit and went back to bed. The poor girl continued to wake up screaming—it seemed like every hour on the hour.

I was emotionally drained by the time an overly cheerful orderly came bopping into my room at 6:00 a.m. "Wake up, Miss Emily. Breakfast is in fifteen down the hall. Group therapy starts at 7:00 a.m., and then you'll meet with your counselor one-on-one." I nodded in return, thinking about Mom and Dad. Where were they? Why weren't they here? My stomach turned when I thought of being in this place alone, obsessing over the wild thought that my parents finally decided to abandon me. I know, maybe somewhat melodramatic. But can you imagine being sixteen and waking up in a psych ward? Believe you me, you start entertaining all kinds of thoughts.

I grabbed my hospital swag bag and headed to the bathroom to brush my teeth. I passed my roommate's bed on the way, tiptoeing past her. She looked peaceful, finally sleeping without interruption.

Looking in the mirror was probably something I shouldn't have done. The dark circles around my eyes were so prominent that they looked pasted on. My skin looked especially pale. I looked sick. And when I remembered where I was, I just wanted to puke.

I shuffled to the meeting lounge, or whatever it was called, in my hospital-issue socks. They itched like a bad case of poison ivy. Another sterile and practically empty room greeted me. A bunch of hard wooden chairs were randomly placed around the linoleum floor, half of them forming a misshapen circle. About fifteen kids my age circulated around the room. Some looked scared. Others looked scary. Some fellow patients seemed cozy with one another. Others, like me, didn't say a word.

After I grabbed some orange juice from the breakfast cart, a man walked in. I recognized him as the counselor who had been with me during the admission process the night before. Though I hadn't been exactly chummy with the guy, his familiar face put me at ease. He seemed safe, like a grounded anchor. And kind.

The counselor directed us to sit down, and so began my first-ever group therapy session. I didn't say one word during the hour but listened intently as others shared traumatic stories about abusive parents, rape, addictions, and actual suicide attempts that left bandaged scars. As these teenagers talked, some angry, others drenched in sad tears, I felt that my problems paled in comparison. Oh sure, I was sad. I was lonely. And I wanted to leave boarding school and go home to be with my mom and dad. All these things had been legitimate issues in my mind, but hearing the horror stories of others shifted my perspective. And I felt the weight of guilt, of being an ungrateful, undeserving little girl.

My parents arrived later that morning. Mom's noisy bangles announced their arrival as she walked down the hallway and into my room. I inhaled her perfume. It worked magic, obliterating, at least temporarily, the antiseptic and mildew stench. Mom looked a little worried but appeared more nonchalant than I would have expected. Maybe she knew she'd freak me out if she burst into hysterics.

She sat on the side of my bed, brushing loose strands of greasy hair out of my eyes and half smiled. "What in the world happened, Emily?" I shrugged my shoulders. I didn't know what to say.

For each solo counseling session during my three-day stay, I don't remember giving some sob story or offering intricate details, a narrow glimpse into my past that would account for some kind of an aha moment for me or the therapist. The mandatory meetings were far from sensational confessions. I was, however, adamant in communicating one fact: I want to go home. I said this like a hundred times, in a hundred different ways. I couldn't be any clearer.

I. Want. To. Go. Home.

When I was officially declared not a danger to myself or others, I was discharged. The counselor had also recommended to my parents that they withdraw me from school and bring me home. "Right now Emily needs your support," he told them. But instead of going to school to pack up my things and head back to Sunset Key with Mom and Dad, I found myself back at Saint Andrew's. To stay.

My parents gave me a handful of reasons why going home was not an option. One, they had already paid my tuition. Two, it was best I finished out the school year in the same place. Yada, yada, yada. When they left, they told me how much they loved and cared for me and all that warm and gooey stuff, but all I heard was, "Sorry, dear, you can't come home with us." And with some hugs, a few words of encouragement to "hang in there, you're fine," and a proverbial slap on the back, I was back in my own world, the one I didn't like very much.

Life resumed its intense pace. No one knew what happened and where I'd been except for some teachers. My peers assumed I simply went home. No one had a clue that I was actually Bakerized. Things went back to normal, my normal, rather quickly. Which meant the same unsettling feelings of discontent and unease overwhelmed me again, pushing me down a deeper tunnel of confusion, loneliness, and depression.

What do I have to do to get out of here? I wondered with such desperation it scared me. But the deeper question, the one that carried even more weight was, *What do I have to do to get my parents to notice me, to show me that they care?* Isn't that what all teenagers want? Some concrete evidence of being loved, wanted, needed, heard? Even though most of us do a poor job of communicating that.

As my emotions swam in endless circles, I thought about getting sick. The Bell's palsy business elicited a lot of compassion from Mom and Dad. But how do I just get sick? What do I do? What do I take?

Pills. That was the first thing that came to mind. *I'm going to take pills.* Seemed like an easy fix. I didn't have access to your serious do-some-damage-in-bulk pills like painkillers or sleep aids. But I did have a full month's supply of Prozac in my handbag. Perfect. I grabbed the bottle and downed four pills with some water. Four. Need me to repeat that?

Four. Low-dose. Antidepressants.

Well, guess what happened after a minute. That's right. Nothing. Epic failure. So therein lay the challenge: determining the right amount of pills to take that would make me seriously ill but wouldn't kill me. Without any resources to help, I'd have to wing it. And wing it I did.

Let me pause for a bit.

As I write this, I'm blown away. I can't believe this actually happened, that I was a depressed teenager thinking that taking excess Prozac was going to solve my problems. It's wild. A part of me almost feels I'm writing about someone else. And as I think back on that time, some scenes are blurred. I don't know if this is true, but I believe some of the haze has to do with God protecting me. If I sat down and thought of every single piece of the puzzle during that time, every single event, every single feeling, every single encounter, every single conversation, every single color, and every single smell, I'd probably have a breakdown.

I don't remember what happened after I tried to figure out the magic number of pills to pop. All I remember is waking up in the emergency room, a thin curtain separating me from the hospital chaos I could hear, but not see. I lay in bed, clutching my stomach after having been forced to drink a charcoal beverage that would help detoxify my body from the bottle of antidepressants I had just ingested an hour or so ago. The drink made me puke immediately, the pitiful bedpan a far cry from an adequate receptacle. I threw up so much, I filled up the commercial-grade waste basket in the corner. A doctor or nurse stuck an IV in me to replenish my body with fluids lost during my nonstop vomiting.

All popping Prozac did for me, once I was physically well enough to leave the ER, was guarantee me another spot in the same psych ward I had visited earlier. Round two was pretty much the same. But this time, Saint Andrew's, who had been in communication with my parents, recommended I leave school and go home.

My exodus from Saint Andrew's happened in what felt like a few seconds. One minute I was walking out of the hospital, feeling the suffocating humidity on my face and watching palm trees yield submissively to the soft breeze. The next I was walking out of the headmaster's office toward my dorm where my parents and I would quickly pack up my belongings and drive a silent four and a half hours to Key West. No one said a word. No one mentioned the pills. The emergency room. That other place. Maybe it was better that way. We could all pretend it never happened.

three

Standing on the dock awaiting the ferry for Sunset Island, while the sun melted my skin and sweat trickled down my neck, I felt relieved. I knew there were logistics that needed to be ironed out, like needing to finish out my junior year at Key West High School, for one, but I didn't care. I was home. To me, no matter what the rest of high school looked like, I finally felt settled. Also, I was used to switching schools so much that the whole new-kid-on-the-block element didn't faze me a bit. I didn't care that I was enrolling in a place where cliques were already formed and long-term bonds were already made and curriculums were already more than halfway completed. I'd manage just fine, thank you very much. Overall, I was in a much better place than a few weeks or even months ago. I closed out the year uneventfully.

When I started my senior year, in a rare surge of courage, I decided to join the tennis team. That's right. Me. The girl who was not created to catch or throw things. I knew some of the players, and the team didn't seem super competitive; I don't even remember the school hosting tryouts. For me tennis was more of a social thing, but when I played, I tried my best to keep the ball in the court, not over the fence or in the adjoining court.

One afternoon, around Thanksgiving, I decided to ditch practice, though I'd already gone through the trouble of changing into my uniform. I knew my mediocre performance wasn't going to suffer drastically because I missed a few drills. So after school I went home and whistled for my border collie, Peaches, who immediately scampered toward me with spirited howls. The two of us took the ferry over to Key West and strolled around A & B Marina, located in the heart of Old Town, which was always bustling with action from incoming and outgoing boats.

I inhaled the saltwater air and paused, with Peaches yapping and yanking the leash, making sure I knew she wasn't happy about the pit stop. As I admired the blanket of sparkling turquoise that stretched in every direction, my eyes fell on an even better sight, one that almost made me drop the leash.

Ricky.

It had been about a year and a half since I'd seen him. My heart pounded, and the palms of my hands started to get sweaty.

With sandy hair tousled from the wind, Ricky hopped off a fishing boat onto the dock. With effortless ease, he flexed his lean muscles to reach back into the boat and drag a cooler out. His dad was there, too, as well as some other guys I didn't recognize. I groaned when I realized I was still wearing my white tennis uniform, also remembering my hair was tied back in a messy ponytail (messy-messy, not cute-messy) and I didn't have a stitch of makeup on. I looked dull and drab. Sigh. This was so not how I saw our reunion happening.

As Peaches yelped beside me, her tail waving furiously,

Ricky turned and our eyes met. I smiled, heart still beating so fast I could hardly catch my breath. I let out a casual but cool, "Oh, hi there! Happy almost Thanksgiving!"

Ricky waved, returning the greeting with his Hollywood grin. "Emily! How are you?" Though he looked happy to see me, my nerves got the best of me and I stammered something like, "Great! Well, okay then. Bye!" So not cool. Mortified by how little girl–like I sounded, I turned away and walked quickly down the dock, dragging a panting Peaches behind me. I'm pretty sure my face at that point was a deep shade of tomato-red.

"Hey, wait up!" Ricky yelled as he dashed toward me, his Rainbow flip-flops beating loudly on the wooden dock. "Are you doing anything tonight?" And then, much to my delight, he asked me if I wanted to hang out.

Not wanting to appear too eager, I feigned a nonchalant, "Sure!" You know, like a fake "whatevs!"

What I didn't know was that right after Ricky and I said our hellos and I walked away, his friend Brian, who was closer to my age, had playfully socked him in the arm and said, "Dude, if you don't ask her out, I will!" Nothing like a little friendly competition, right? Well, that was all the motivation Ricky needed to come after me and corral me for a date. Not that I needed much corralling.

That night we ate at Shula's, a steakhouse hot spot. One of the first things Ricky told me after we sat down was that he knew I had been lying all along. I figured as much. After all, his parents were aware of the truth, so why wouldn't they tell him? Still, his admission brought a sense of relief. It was nice to have a conversation and really get to know each other without me trying to keep up with stupid lies.

While I had been jittery getting ready for our date, most of my anxiety disappeared the moment I took my seat at the dinner table. Ricky's laid-back, warm personality set me at ease. He was funny, making hilarious comments as he munched on breadsticks and we sipped on Cokes. When our food came, even though it looked and smelled delicious, I didn't want to eat. I didn't want to entertain the embarrassing possibility of getting a sliver of beef or a strand of spinach stuck in my teeth. Then again, not eating would probably look just as dumb. So I indulged in the mouthwatering entrée without regret.

I loved that I could be myself around Ricky. I wasn't a bit shy and welcomed being able to be silly. Though we'd had a good time at breakfast a year and a half earlier, we were more comfortable with each other this time around. Our connection was apparent. I flirted and gave off giggly smiles, and Ricky sat close to me, asking a million questions, his hand on mine during dessert. When we left the restaurant in time to make my 11:00 p.m. curfew, I noticed he grabbed a box of matches with the venue's logo on it and shoved it in his back jeans pocket.

Ricky was home from Charlotte, visiting his parents over Thanksgiving after the final NASCAR race at the Homestead-Miami Speedway. He had only a few more days left before he had to head back home. We became an item that night and took advantage of practically every minute before he left.

For the next few days, Ricky and I took walks along the beach, sat and watched the sunset, and had romantic dinners. I know it sounds cliché, but we could talk about anything—and we did. We compared our tastes in music. We talked about our families. We shared our dreams. We opened up about things we hadn't told anyone before. It wasn't long after those memorable first few days together that I told him the truth about being hospitalized twice when I was at Saint Andrew's. He didn't act shocked or look at me like I was a nut; he was kind and compassionate. Ricky didn't have a judgmental bone in his body. Forgive me if this sounds cheesy, but because he was such a gentleman, respectful and sweet, he was the first person I had ever met who emulated the love of Jesus.

I was in tears when Ricky, my first real boyfriend, left for Charlotte, both of us promising to call and think about each other every day, which we faithfully did. For the rest of my senior year, he was all I could think about. I was falling in love, fast and hard. Though I had made a few friends, I didn't spend my final months of high school partying with them or dreaming about prom or getting excited about the senior class trip. I had Ricky on the brain. While we were apart, he helped pass the time until we could see each other again by writing me long letters and brightening up many of my days with surprise bouquets of exotic flowers.

Ricky flew me to Charlotte on Super Bowl weekend 2004, when the Carolina Panthers fought against and (sadly) were defeated by the New England Patriots. Not much of a football fan—I still don't even know what a pass rush or a blitz is—I was more excited about the fact that it was my birthday and I was turning eighteen! Not only would I celebrate becoming a legal adult, I was doing so with the love of my life.

That weekend, Ricky threw me a surprise party at his house, a spacious and relatively empty bachelor pad that resembled a Gothic castle. There was only one thing that stood out to me as odd—his choice of artwork. Smack in the middle of the living room was a large framed picture of a fish that was purchased, as indicated by a label, at the local Bass Pro Shop. Well, I did say it was a bachelor pad.

Ricky and I enjoyed a candlelit dinner at the Palm. Afterward, as we pulled up to his place, I noticed a barrage of parked cars lined up and down the streets. "Your neighbors must be having a party," I remarked, then he playfully nudged me in the ribs as we made our way toward the front door. "Hey, wait a minute! How come we weren't invited?" Ricky didn't say a word in response, offering only his trademark boyish grin.

Imagine my surprise when he threw open the door and there, within a sea of hundreds of pink streamers and balloons, stood about fifty people, drinks in hand, screaming, "Surprise!" This was classic Ricky. He always pulled out the red carpet for me, doing thoughtful and romantic things, going out of his way to make me feel special.

A few weeks later, I met Ricky's sister, Lynne, and her husband, Marshall. Though I had already met Mr. and Mrs. Hendrick and seen them around Key West, it was my first time meeting Lynne and the first official sit-down dinner with all of us. I had been at the track with Ricky all day and was dressed casually in flip-flops and comfortable, worn jeans. The dinner was a spur-of-the-moment event, so while I balked at first, since I looked like I'd just woken up and was headed to the neighborhood convenience store for some milk, well, what was I going to do? As it turned out, my outfit was a nonissue and I passed with flying colors. Which just means that I didn't spill anything during dinner, accidently break or stain anything in the house, or blurt out something really dumb or inappropriate at dinner. And, oh yeah, my biggest accolade was I didn't get any part of dinner unknowingly stuck in my teeth. Go me!

Leaving Charlotte to go back to Florida was sad, but two weeks later, Ricky flew me to the Daytona 500, the Super Bowl of NASCAR, for my first race. Obviously I was stoked to see him, but I was also psyched to get an inside look at the NASCAR racing scene. As a newbie, I didn't know what to expect. I knew I'd probably be right about one thing though. I guessed it was going to be loud. Very loud.

Ricky had retired from racing in 2002 after injuring his shoulder in an accident. He then became a spotter for driver Brian Vickers, the 2003 Nationwide Series champion and also one of Ricky's closest friends. Because race cars are driven at astronomical speeds without side or rearview mirrors, spotters act as mirrors, making drivers aware of blind spots and keeping them up-to-date with what is happening around the track. Spotters are positioned high above the track and are in constant communication with the driver via two-way radio. While Ricky wasn't doing his thing on the track, we spent time together in the bus.

My experience at Daytona was quite different than that of a typical fan who'd likely be one of tens of thousands of fans navigating through the maze of vendors and food stands, tailgating in ingenious ways, or watching the race in the packed stands. Because NASCAR teams are constantly on the road traveling from track to track all over the country, owners and drivers usually fly or drive to the race venue and stay in their private, and quite lavish, tour-like buses on the infield, smack in the middle of the track, or sometimes in secure and heavily guarded designated lots near the track. Ricky worked and I hung out in the bus, watching the race on a TV screen. The bus became almost like a second home.

Daytona was bigger than I had ever imagined. The place was a madhouse, not to mention celebrity filled. President George W. Bush was in attendance, as well as Ben Affleck, Whoopi Goldberg, and LeAnn Rimes. That year, Dale Earnhardt Jr. won the race, exactly six years after his father, Dale Earnhardt Sr., won his. And though I wasn't seated with the die-hard fans in the stands on the opposite side of the tracks, their enthusiasm and energy was so palpable they gave the monstrous roars of the powerful race-car engines a run for their money.

As graduation day approached, I juggled a few options. I wanted to take a year off, to give myself a break from school and take time to think about my future. Honestly the thought of having to struggle through more years of textbooks, papers, formulas, and exams gave me headaches. Also, I didn't know what I wanted to be or do when I grew up. And that wasn't something I was going to magically stumble upon the second my principal slapped a diploma in my hand.

When I mentioned to Dad the idea of taking time off, he just about came unglued. "You are going to school, young lady!" For a minute, probably not longer than two, I considered enrolling in a college in Charleston, South Carolina, or attending the University of North Carolina in Charlotte so I could be closer to you-know-who. The more Ricky and I talked, however, the more it seemed the natural next step should be to move to Charlotte, minus the whole college experience. This was something I really, really, really wanted to do. My heart belonged to Ricky. So a month or two before graduation, I told Mom and Dad about my plans to move to Charlotte. Oh, and I'm not proud to admit this, but I also threw out a "If you don't help me get an apartment there, I guess I'll just have to move in with my boyfriend." Though he and my mom loved Ricky like their own son, Dad especially was horrified at the thought of his daughter shacking up. But he didn't take me that seriously and shrugged off my plans. Poor Dad. He totally underestimated the will of a stubborn young woman in love.

Ricky was with me the day I graduated from Key West. After the pomp and circumstance, we went to my house to pack up my stuff. When I said I was moving after graduation, I meant, like, that day. When Dad saw Ricky sprinting down the stairs hauling two big boxes in his arms, Dad was flabbergasted.

"Emily!" he barked as Ricky gulped and froze on the staircase. Quite the tough guy, my dad always had a way of intimidating Ricky, though Ricky was always extra careful to be respectful and considerate toward Dad.

Glaring at the two of us, my father shook his head in disapproval. "What is going on?"

Sheepish, Ricky looked at me with questioning eyes. I knew what he was thinking. *Uh, should I take these boxes back to your room and nix our whole plan?*

I stood my ground at the top of the steps. "Dad, I told you I was leaving!"

Dad stood still for a few seconds, fuming on the inside and staring at Ricky and me without saying a word. Finally he threw his hands up in surrender. "Fine," he muttered, a twinge of self-defeat coating his voice. "We'll get you an apartment."

Even without crystalline beaches, mouthwatering sunsets, and white sand as pure as sugar, Charlotte has a beauty of its own—and a lot more cars than fishing boats. Dad rented an apartment for me right down the street from where Ricky lived, in the South Park neighborhood of the city. South Park is a shopping mecca, home to a variety of upscale restaurants, trendy boutiques, eclectic cafés, and the largest mall in all of North Carolina. (Not that I ever stayed in my own place. A fact I'm not proud of, but hey, it's the truth.)

Ricky and I started building a life together. We were together all the time. He owned a local motorcycle shop in Pineville, and we'd ride one of his bikes out to local burger joints to find the best-tasting cheeseburger in town. We went to the Bahamas on vacation, and true to both our homebody natures, we'd lie around the pool and beach, soaking in the rays and enjoying the tranquility. Come sunset, we'd spread beach towels out by the surf and gaze at the sky, bold colors of orange, red, and purple overlapping the horizon while luke-warm salt water swept over our feet.

Ricky was my best friend. I had never shared so much of myself, my dreams, my struggles with anyone else. During a particular rough patch Ricky knew how much I needed my mom. I missed her so badly. Mom was a lifeline to home. Knowing I was especially homesick one weekend, Ricky flew my mother and me out to Miami for a few days of rest and relaxation, our schedule consisting only of shopping and spa treatments. It was just what I needed.

Most weekends, Thursday through Sunday, were spent

on the NASCAR circuit. We'd travel to places like Talladega, Michigan, New Hampshire, Chicagoland (fun fact: it's not actually in the city of Chicago but in Joliet, an hour away), and, of course, famed Daytona. Outside of small distinguishing features among the tracks, city locations, and fluctuating emotions from the team depending on wins and losses, every weekend was pretty much the same. We'd arrive at the race location on Thursday night, Ricky would spend most of Friday practicing on the track, and at night we'd grill out, sometimes hanging out with the drivers and their families or girlfriends. Saturday and Sunday were race days, and when it was all over, we'd fly back home to Charlotte. While Ricky did his business on the track, I didn't mind being alone on the bus. It was relaxing. I've always had an independent streak and enjoyed my solitude. Sometimes I'd watch the races or get together with the wives or girlfriends of other drivers, or if I was feeling particularly motivated, whip out a rag and some Windex or Lysol and clean up.

Ricky and I had talked seriously about marriage on several occasions and even visited the Hendricks' family jeweler with his mom to pick out a ring. When the NASCAR season was over, Ricky, who wasn't the world's best secret-keeper, told me he planned on proposing to me in Saint Bart's. I think one of the reasons he told me was because I had always feared he'd asked me to marry him at some NASCAR event, which would have been, of course, so unromantic. As much as I enjoyed the racing sport, I didn't want a proposal associated with roaring engines, earplugs, and the stench of hot dogs and fuel. Ricky respected my wishes and promised he'd wait to get down on one knee until after the season was over. When he mentioned

Saint Bart's, I begged him to stop telling me his plans. I mean, really, a girl's got to be surprised, right? Around this same time, we started making plans to build a house nearby in the same South Park neighborhood and moved into a small condo to save some money while the house was being built. Ricky warned me we'd probably be living in sleeping bags for a few months, but I didn't care. As long as he was with me, I'd do just fine living in a tent in the woods if I had to.

One of the things I admired about Ricky was his faith. While he didn't shout his beliefs from a rooftop or announce them to everyone he met, he had a quiet but resilient faith in God. He loved to pray with me. Simple prayers, nothing elaborate or long-winded. I remember the first time he took my hand at dinner and said, "Let's bless the food." Okay, so initially I thought it was weird, mainly because I'd never done that before. Nor had I been with anyone who would ever consider "blessing the food." But it felt personal, and real.

Ricky even prayed with me at times outside of meals. I'll never forget flying on a little plane over the mountains after visiting my grandparents in rural Kentucky. The wind lashed out violently at the small aircraft, bouncing us in every direction but straight. The plane would swing from side to side, then plummet fast and furious a couple of feet. I had never been so scared in my life. I dug my nails into the armrests while Ricky whispered a prayer. "Keep us safe, God." And almost as fast as those words were spoken, an indescribable peace beset my heart. I was no longer afraid.

At my core, I wanted to deepen my faith beyond "save me" prayers and simply following Ricky's lead. I wanted to know God as something other than a whimsical being in the sky. But I didn't know how. I didn't even know what it meant. Ricky and I would sometimes attend church at the track, and when we were in Charlotte on Sundays, we'd accompany Mr. and Mrs. Hendrick to their home church, Central Church of God.

I'll never forget the life-changing experience I had at a service one Sunday right after I moved to Charlotte. The pastor gave a moving message. I don't remember what he said, but I'll never forget how I felt. Goosebumps shivered up and down my spine as the pastor gave an altar call to anyone who wanted more of God, who wanted a deeper faith, who felt His presence. Something stirred inside my spirit, something similar to what I experienced at the youth retreat some six years earlier. As the worship band played quietly in the background and I could hear the soft commotion of men and women, young and old, taking slow strides down the aisles of the spacious church, Ricky grabbed my hand. I gave it a tight squeeze, but he didn't just want to hold it. He stood up and started making his way down to the aisle, still gripping my hand.

We stood at the front of the altar, shoulder to shoulder with a handful of other people, including Ricky's uncle John, president of Hendrick Motor Sports, and prayed quietly. I had never before felt any shift of emotion in church. When I used to attend Mass with my parents, I'd always just sit and stare at the priest with a blank expression on my face, thinking about where we were going to go after church or what we would eat or what TV show was on later that night or that I should actually start studying for my math test or whether or not the boy down the block liked me. Sitting in church was nothing more than a means to an end—usually just getting it over with so I could move on to more fun things, things that actually mattered to me.

But standing next to Ricky at the front of Central Church of God, I felt the love of God wrap around me. It wasn't just an emotional feeling. I actually felt squeezed tight. I knew the Spirit was moving in me, beckoning me in His gentleman way to dig deeper. To get to know Him.

Looking back, though I considered myself a Christian, sadly it was more of a label I pinned loosely on my identity than an actual relationship with God, a genuine faith that takes root in your spirit and guides your every decision. I mean, I was living with my boyfriend, for Pete's sake, not a very spiritual thing to do—and not a decision I'm proud of.

But I know now that even when we plod through life, making mistakes along the way, trying to figure out what faith is and what it means and why it matters, God uses each and every circumstance, and yes, even every mistake, to plot a course that ultimately will lead straight into His arms.

Anne Lamott opened her book *Traveling Mercies* this way:

My coming to faith did not start with a leap but rather a series of staggers from what seemed like one safe place to another. Like lily pads, round and green, these places summoned and then held me up while I grew. Each prepared me for the next leaf on which I would land, and in this way I moved across the swamp of doubt and fear. When I look back at some of these early resting places . . . I can see how flimsy and indirect a path they made. Yet each step brought me closer to the verdant pad of faith on which I somehow stay afloat today.[*]

Oh, how I can relate! Crying in a sleeping bag on a gymnasium floor, holding hands with my soon-to-be fiancé as the Spirit of God slowly began to build an awareness of His presence in my heart—those were just a couple of my resting places. I'd bounce and slip my way through more lily pads—making a ton of mistakes along the way—but even in the moments when I didn't make the best choices and opted for the easy path instead of the narrow one, God would always be with me, waiting until I finally surrendered wholeheartedly to Him. Until I finally realized and confessed that my life, my desires, and my ultimate identity would never be complete until they'd be found in Him.

That Sunday I remember saying thank you to God over and over and over. Those were the only two words that came naturally, easily, from the depths of my heart. As the pastor prayed over us, I remember feeling strongly that God had given me Ricky as a gift. And I felt in that moment—I'm not sure why—a strong and comforting sense of God saying to me, *Emily, everything is going to be okay.*

In October 2004, after a race in Charlotte, Ricky, his mom, and I headed off to beautiful Maui for a break. It was great to be able to spend some quality time with Mrs. Hendrick, to

---

[*] Anne Lamott, *Traveling Mercies: Some Thoughts on Faith* (New York: Random House, 1999), 3.

continue to get to know her better. Together the three of us enjoyed some great dinners and occasional sightseeing, and Ricky and I spent a lot of quality time just the two of us.

This trip included some of my most memorable moments with Ricky. When we had spent time together in Key West or some other vacation spot like the Bahamas, we were lazy. We didn't do much other than lay out on the beach or by the pool. This trip was different. We did it all.

We went snorkeling, holding hands with our faces plunged into the water, where we could see schools of rainbow-colored tropical fish brushing past us along with bright pink, orange, and gold coral reefs rhythmically swaying with the current underneath us in an underwater paradise. We even woke up one morning just before four—okay, so I didn't really "wake" up; more like Ricky pounded on my door and dragged me out of bed—so we could take a sunrise helicopter tour of Haleakalā, Maui's inactive volcano. As the aircraft whirred off in the dark about an hour before dawn, I was half asleep, forcing myself to stay awake and show some enthusiasm, especially since Ricky was beside himself in the sleek machine.

Sometime after 6:00 a.m., we approached the rim of the volcano, which climbed an impressive 10,023 feet above sea level. It was then I was jolted awake by the sky's majestic beauty. I cannot even put into words how I felt as dawn began to unfold with multiple shades of morning glory. When Mark Twain visited Haleakalā in 1866, he wrote it was "the sublimest spectacle I ever witnessed, and I think the memory of it will remain with me always."** Preach it, brother!

** Mark Twain, *Roughing It*, Project Gutenberg eBook, part 8, August 18, 2006, http://www.gutenberg.org/files/3177/old/orig3177-h/3177-h.htm.

At one point, the helicopter hovered a little too close to the edge of the volcano for my comfort. Convinced we were going to hit it, I started having heart palpitations. Knowing my fear of flying and without me needing to say a word, Ricky grabbed my sweaty hand, loudly reassuring me over the deafening engine with a wide grin on his face, "Relax, Em. The pilot knows what he's doing. We are not, I repeat not, going to crash into the volcano." He squeezed my hand tight and with an encouraging grin he shook his head and laughed this time, putting to rest my obviously silly fears. "Trust me, that would never happen." On the flight back to the hotel, we enjoyed a bird's-eye view of lush rainforests and towering sea cliffs along the rugged coastline.

Looking back on this vacation, I realize what a gift from God it was. Trips like this were few and far between, and every memory captured was special. I know it's impossible to live every day on vacation, free of stress, worry, and rocky roads. Life isn't a fairy tale; I would learn that soon enough. But to have shared pieces of paradise, which in the big picture were as fleeting as a breath, means the world to me. Since the beginning of our relationship, and particularly on this trip, Ricky had brought out in me a sense of adventure, of possibility, of hope—parts of me that would soon disappear in a slow fade.

On October 24, 2004, Ricky, who was taking helicopter lessons at the time, was scheduled to fly a copter to the Martinsville Speedway. The weather wasn't cooperating and so he, along with his uncle John and his twin cousins, Kimberly and

Jennifer Hendrick; general manager Jeff Turner; chief engine builder Randy Dorton; Joe Jackson, a DuPont executive; and Scott Lathram, a pilot for driver Tony Stewart, boarded a private plane piloted by Richard Tracy and Elizabeth Morrison and took off for the short flight.

I felt like I was getting the first symptoms of the flu, so I stayed behind, which was rare. But there was something else that kept me home, something I have never before shared publicly.

Ricky and I had just gotten into a heated argument before he left the house. I don't remember the reason for the unkind words we spat at each other, but our conversation wasn't pretty. I'm sure I was at fault. I'm aware, very aware, of my strong stubborn streak, which in this case could have very well fueled the argument.

Ricky and I made a pact when we started dating. If we were ever going somewhere without the other, we promised to at least call or text to let each other know we arrived safely. It didn't have to be a long message, just a simple "I made it. Talk soon. Love you."

Ricky was scheduled to land that morning. But I didn't get a call. Or a message. And still nothing even after I tried calling him every few minutes, leaving what seemed like fifty messages that said, "I don't know where you are. I know we didn't leave on the best terms, but at least call me back. Or text me. Something. Where are you?" I was getting frustrated. Was he really that mad?

As the hours passed without a word, I became anxious. But I still waited. For a phone call that would never come.

four

I sat on the living room couch, flipping through TV channels I wasn't paying attention to and thumbing through magazine articles that looked like an incomprehensible jumble of vowels and consonants. The distractions were pointless. Why does time seem to stand still when you're waiting?

Finally, my phone rang. My heart raced. I grabbed the vibrating phone so quickly that it almost flew out of my hand.

It was Ricky's mother. Disappointed, I let out a sigh as I said, "Oh, Mrs. Hendrick."

"Emily." Her voice was firm and calm, but betrayed concern. "I need you to go to Lynne's house right now." There was an emphasis on the last two words.

I didn't respond right away. I just knew something was wrong. Heart racing, stomach tightening, I felt like I was going to throw up. "Okay," I heard myself saying, as if a part of me was already beginning to detach.

The problem was I didn't know how to get to Lynne's house. I'd been there a few times with Ricky, but I had never paid attention to what turns were made when or where. I didn't even know my way around Charlotte yet. Mrs. Hendrick hung up the phone before I had a chance to ask for Lynne's address, so I drove off and hoped for the best. Somehow I found myself pulling into her driveway mere minutes after the phone call ended. There's no other way to say this—I truly believe God guided me there.

Though Lynne was expecting me, she didn't know what was going on either. We waited, mostly in silence, for her husband, who we were told had more information, to get home. When Marshall walked through the door, his face looked pale. Before Lynne or I had a chance to assault him with questions, he spoke, barely above a whisper. "The plane is missing."

Everything froze in that moment. Shock slowly invaded my heart, my mind. I shook my head and defiantly looked directly into Marshall's eyes. "No. No, that can't be true."

A missing plane is not a good thing. And while it suggested that the plane had crashed, I refused to believe that. I refused to even consider what was probably a tragic reality. I still believed Ricky was okay. I mean, Marshall hadn't said the word *crash*, nor had he offered us any actual evidence, so as far as I was concerned, the pilot probably had to do an emergency landing or maybe his radar stopped working. "Missing" had to mean something other than gone forever. It had to.

While disbelief overwhelmed me when I heard Marshall say those four words, at the same time a heavy sadness fell upon me. I felt like every bone, fiber, tissue, nerve, and muscle in my body had turned into concrete. And there I was. Swinging between denial and pain. Pain and denial. As Marshall, Lynne, and I drove over to the Hendricks', no one saying a word, conflicting emotions began to claw their way through me.

Still trying to wrap my brain around what a missing plane

meant, I wanted solid answers. I wanted to talk to someone who knew what was going on. I didn't want to come up with a million definitions of what a missing plane meant or sit like some helpless puppet imagining a handful of worst-case scenarios. I wanted the truth.

I thought about the argument Ricky and I had right before he left for the airport. The unkind words. My pride. For the life of me I couldn't remember what we had fought about. What was so darn important that demanded our good-byes in a fit of fury? What did I want? What was I trying to say? What was I holding on to so tight that I couldn't switch gears? Regret became my new companion.

The mood at the Hendricks' was tense, somber. Mrs. Hendrick's eyes were red and swollen as she made her way, everyone else in tow, inside the home office. I still didn't know what was going on and felt dreadfully out of place. Like a lost puppy, I followed the trail of family members. One by one, we formed a circle and held hands while the Hendricks' pastor led us in a heartfelt prayer.

I only half listened to his words. I was still wondering if there was an update, if the plane had been found, when I heard, injected somewhere in the prayer for comfort and strength, "Nobody had made it."

Nobody had made it.

My body went limp, releasing my grip from whoever's hand I was holding at the time. Nobody had told me that no one had made it. That Ricky hadn't made it. That he was gone. I began to drown in a sea of rage, violently pitched against massive waves, unable to gain my footing, let alone breathe.

I was angry. The rage blinding. Had I been the only one

in the room who didn't know the news? Really? I was angry at God, tuning out the pastor's prayer directed to a deity in that moment I wasn't sure even existed. If God was real, then I didn't like Him. He obviously didn't think much of me. When the final "amen" was spoken, I stood invisible, staring at a group of people consoling one another through smothering sobs and weighted embraces.

During the course of the next hour or so, I learned details. The Hendricks' private plane had crashed into the Bull Mountains, only seven miles from the airport where they were scheduled to land. No one on board had a chance to survive.

The waiting was over. The worst had come.

While I took the Hendricks up on their offer to stay with them for a few days, later that night I headed to the condo to pick up a few things—the condo where Ricky and I had been living together just twenty-four hours previously.

It was dark when I walked in. Quiet. Everything was in place, as if life hadn't changed. As if my world hadn't been turned upside down. I waited in the stillness, shutting my eyes, praying that when I opened them, Ricky would be standing beside me, playfully asking what I was doing standing with my eyes closed. Nothing was different when I opened my eyes. Ricky was still gone.

I walked slowly around the place, dazed. I could still smell Ricky's cologne. I saw the bowl of cereal he had for breakfast in the kitchen sink, milk still in it. I brushed past his toothbrush lying on the bathroom counter, still smelling of mint. I noticed his laundry on the bedroom dresser, still waiting to be put away, clothes he'd never wear again. Denial crept its way in again and I panicked. *What if they are wrong? What if*

Ricky's still out there? What if he's hurt? What if he's waiting for us to come find him?

As quickly as I could, I shoved some toiletries and clothes into an overnight bag. I didn't want to stay long. As comforting as it was seeing signs of Ricky all over our home, it was equally just as crushing. Before I left, I remember grabbing a teen Bible from inside my night table. I had never read it before, nor did I know how to read it. But as I held the book in my trembling hands, I felt something or maybe even Someone nudging me to flip through the pages. For what? I wondered. To read mumbo-jumbo stuff that was written thousands of years ago by stuffy religious folk who hadn't just tragically lost a loved one? What comfort could I possibly find? What words to make this all go away? What verse to make Ricky walk through the door?

This particular Bible offered topical studies on subjects like dating, purpose, relationships, and self-esteem. When I closed my eyes, book in hand, I prayed, "God, give me a sign. Give me something." I didn't have a particular sign or a particular something in mind. I just wanted evidence, proof that God was with me. Proof that God cared. Proof that this wasn't a perverse joke, a sick and twisted abuse of divine power. Proof that God didn't just obliterate the love of my life and nine others, leaving a trail of grieving loved ones behind, simply just because.

I played Bible roulette and randomly opened to a page that blared a bold heading, "How to Deal with Death." My eyes skimmed through a paragraph about heaven, about our souls belonging to God, about the Holy Spirit being available to us as a comforter, about how near to the brokenhearted God is. And then I read the words of Jesus: "Do not let your hearts be troubled. You believe in God; believe also in me. My Father's house has many rooms; if that were not so, would I have told you that I am going there to prepare a place for you? And if I go and prepare a place for you, I will come back and take you to be with me that you also may be where I am. You know the way to the place where I am going" (John 14:1–4 NIV).

I can't tell you that reading those words immediately made me feel better. I can't tell you the tears stopped. And I can't tell you that the heavy weight of loss was lifted. What I did feel was confirmation of God's presence. He was with me. Silent, perhaps. Maybe even somewhat distant. But as I stumbled through the shifting emotions of numbing shock, insufferable sadness, and seething anger, a part of me was assured that God hadn't abandoned me.

The days before the funeral were a blur. I retreated into the shadows as Ricky's immediate family members spun in a flurry of phone calls. Of making arrangements. Of blocking out schedules. You know, logistics. When something traumatic happens, the world doesn't stop. You can't just bury your head in the sand without doing what needs to be done. Eulogies and obituaries need to be written. Programs created. Ministers called. Service details relayed. I can't even begin to imagine what Ricky's parents were going through, needing to finalize the last pieces of his life while their hearts were exploding.

I camped out in the Hendricks' guest room most of the time, aware that though Ricky and I were going to get married, I wasn't officially family. I didn't feel like I fit in or even deserved to be there. I never felt so alone in my life. Maybe I was overly insecure or so consumed with losing the love of my life, but I felt out of place, wearing the insignificant, temporary label of "girlfriend." Though deep down I knew it wasn't true, it felt almost parallel to a fling. This feeling would come and go during the course of the next few months, sometimes even making me question whether or not our relationship was real. It's mind-boggling how grief can doctor, even contaminate, your thoughts.

The night before the funeral, in a rare moment of intimate quiet, Mrs. Hendrick and I sat on her living room couch. Tears slipped down my cheeks as I stared out the windows that surrounded the room. The view was empty, pitch-black, void of even a hint of moonlight. I looked at her with a sadness only she could understand and asked, not really expecting an answer, "When will I stop hurting?"

Mrs. Hendrick looked at me with eyes of compassion, understanding the fullness of loss, of pain, of emptiness. As she cupped my hands in hers, she began to pray. I had always admired the strength and grace she drew from her faith. As she prayed over me, I felt the Holy Spirit moving in my own spirit. His presence was unmistakable, covering me with a feeling of settling warmth. Mrs. Hendrick prayed that I would know God, that I would experience His peace, His hope.

I'd been prayed over before, and though I'm not thrilled to admit this, most times I'd zoned out, thinking about things other than God. But when Mrs. Hendrick prayed, I devoured her words. I wanted so badly what she was praying over me. And in that moment, I knew God wanted me to have it, too, to have a deeper connection, a relationship with Him other than showing up at church services or praying occasional glib sentences. I didn't know it, but this moment was another drawing me toward God, another step in the long journey of finally coming home.

During the funeral services, which celebrated the lives of all ten people aboard the plane, I sat in the front row of the Central Church of God. The same church where Ricky and I had visited together, the same church where we both experienced a move of God during an altar call. Hundreds of black-clad mourners, family and friends, gathered together that morning, filling every seat in the large church. Beautiful words were spoken, thousands of tears shed.

As the scene that surrounded me faded into a muffled background, I stared at the large picture of Ricky that was placed in his honor at the front of the church. My eyes trailed over each feature of his beautiful face. His Romanesque nose. His winning smile. His perfect teeth. My body sat rigid in the pew, immobile, while on the inside I screamed, *No, no, no! This isn't happening! This isn't real!*

I was mad as I stared at the photo of Ricky. Mad at him for leaving me. Mad at God for taking him. Mad at Ricky's sister for not mentioning my name as she spoke eloquently of Ricky's life. Mad at myself whenever I remembered the last conversation Ricky and I had, filled with regret at how I allowed anger and pride to stand in the way of peace.

I was mad when the funeral came to a close and I was offered what sounded like empty or generic condolences. Nobody could say anything right. I was so angry at how Ricky's life was cut so tragically short that I wanted to punch anyone in the face who said trite platitudes such as:

"Everything happens for a reason."

"Ricky's in a better place."

"Now he's your guardian angel."

"You're so young, you'll find another man before you know it."

I was mad that those who knew these ten people only from a distance could go home and resume their normal lives and nothing would change. Oh, I was sure they'd be sad. But they wouldn't nurse wounds that would never completely heal. I watched Mrs. Hendrick walk over to Ricky's photo, sobbing as she reached her trembling arms around the wooden frame, holding on for dear life. My heart tore in two, watching the outpouring of grief of a mother who had just lost her only son.

The next day, my eyes slowly opened as the light of dawn peeked through the window. For a split second I forgot where I was. Then I remembered. I was alone. Ricky was gone, never coming back. I would wake up every morning like this, without him. The only way to describe the emptiness was that I felt I was drowning in a pit. I sobbed into the pillow, so hard I could barely catch my breath. All I could think about was his absence and what that meant. Ricky wouldn't call anymore. He wouldn't be there to tell me he loved me and that I mattered. The dream we had of being together forever, of creating a life of our own, was over. My anchor, my life. Gone.

This was when I really did want to die. A part of me genuinely believed I would be next. It wasn't theatrics, but a simple, matter-of-fact resignation. There was no way that God would take Ricky away just to leave me on earth by myself. I remember sharing this with my mom, who stayed with me for a few days after the crash. She got so angry whenever I'd mention wanting to die. "Emily, stop. Stop the nonsense. Don't say those things," she'd plead with me. Mom tried her best to comfort me, not saying much with words but a lot with her presence. I leaned on her so much during that time. While there wasn't anything she could say or do to bring Ricky back, which was all I wanted, she was there. And to me, that meant the world. There's nothing like having your mama around when your world collapses.

Dad, too, came up but just for the day of the funeral. He had to head back home. Key West was celebrating Fantasy Fest, the Mardi Gras of Florida, and they had company scheduled to come to town. On Friday, two days after the funeral, I lay in bed back in my apartment that had been relatively empty since I had moved to Charlotte. Mom slept in the other bedroom. A wave of nausea suddenly hit me and I stumbled my way into the bathroom, saying hello (and good-bye) to the chicken dinner my mother had forced me to eat the night before.

As I reeled in dizziness and plopped down on the floor next to the toilet after there was absolutely nothing remaining in my stomach, it dawned on me that I hadn't had a period in a while. My brain spun. *Could it be? Maybe my body is just reacting from the stress.* Maybe this. Maybe that. I tried to rationalize away the obvious. Then, in a split-second mental shift, I remembered that the Hendricks had asked me to come over in an hour or so; Ricky's ashes were going to be delivered.

It felt like a sucker punch. Just when you think you've accepted a painful reality—after hearing the initial bad news, after sitting at a funeral, after waking up alone, after your mind focuses attention elsewhere—something else happens, another painful reminder that the one you love is gone. This reminded me of my trip to Starbucks the day before. As I waited for my coffee, I caught a glimpse of the daily paper on a stand next to a decorative barrel of coffee. The crash was on the front page. Pictures. In the brief glance I stole, I couldn't see details of the charred wreckage, but I saw trees. Lots of them. The photo was filled with trees colored by autumn, bursts of gold, spice, and burgundy. And then I saw it. Smack in the middle of the beautiful foliage, a depression. Downed trees. Mangled rubble. Twisted metal.

Staring at the photo of the crash, I felt physical pain throughout my body, as though a hundred knives were stabbing me repeatedly. It was the first and only time I had seen a picture of the crash. And it prompted me to think about what had happened the second the plane plowed into the side of the mountain. Was Ricky in pain? Did he know what was coming? Was he scared? I stood in a trance, staring blindly at the barista who held my coffee in her hand, nodding at me to take it. But all I could do was stand there and think about Ricky. And as I numbly walked out of Starbucks, without the latte I had already paid for, I realized I was only torturing myself thinking about those morbid details. I had to believe that God took Ricky immediately. That upon impact, God took him home, that Ricky's physical body instantaneously turned into ashes. Back to its beginnings.

That morning I told Mrs. Hendrick I'd stop over later. Besides the fact I didn't feel well, I was hurt. The other day I'd asked her for a bit of Ricky's ashes, just enough to fill a locket for a necklace. She'd said no. The answer crushed me, especially because it took so much courage to even ask. I'm sure she had her reasons, but whatever they were, it still made me feel rejected, less than.

Mom wasn't awake yet, so I tiptoed my way out of my apartment and headed to the local drugstore for a pregnancy test.

When I came back, she was making some coffee or something. She offered a warm smile and said, "Good morning, Emily." I sped past her toward the bathroom. Sensing I probably needed some space, my mother let me be.

For a long time I sat holding the shopping bag to my chest, entertaining a barrage of wild thoughts. Of fear, worry, concern.

I'm only eighteen.

I can't have a baby.

I can't deal with this right now.

I can't do this by myself.

Being a teen mom wasn't part of the plan.

As I ripped open the package and held the test in my hand, another thought cast an even bigger shadow. *What if I'm not pregnant?* That thought terrified me the most.

I waited a long two minutes for the results, breathing through the rising panic in my chest. I wanted a baby. I knew it right then. No doubt about it. A child was something to look forward to, a gift from Ricky, a piece of him that would be mine. I stared into the tiny window of that five-inch piece of plastic, the dye slowly taking shape. When the positive sign appeared fully, I felt the greatest delight. I was in fact having a baby.

Unfortunately, my elation didn't last long. I started wrestling with the fear of it being a false positive. Maybe it was a bad test. Maybe I didn't follow the directions correctly. Maybe I left it out too soon or read the sign wrong. Feeling overwhelmed, I knew it was time to get Mom. When I told her the news after I quietly stepped out of the bathroom, she stood silent with her mouth open.

"Oh my," Mom finally said, bewildered. And then a smile curled on her face as she reached out and drew me into her arms.

Hesitant to accept what was good news, I quickly interrupted our moment of happy. "But, uh, I don't know. Maybe the test is wrong or something." As always, I needed proof. I needed to be sure, absolutely-without-a-shadow-of-a-doubt sure.

"Why don't we see a doctor, Emily?" Mom suggested. "So you can know for sure."

I called my doctor, who also happened to be the Hendricks' family doctor, to see if he could squeeze me in sometime that day. Sensing alarm in my voice, he told me to come right away. "Go through the back door," he suggested, respecting my privacy and not wanting to cause an unnecessary scene.

Less than an hour later, after receiving a warm greeting from the doctor and waiting in a nondescript exam room for a nurse to draw some blood, I sat in the doctor's personal office, waiting. Waiting for results. Waiting for my future.

And then, as the doctor took a seat in front of me, came the three best words I'd heard that week: "Yup, you're pregnant!"

Elation. That's all I can say. Absolute elation. Though I'd been steeped in tears all week, feeling tears of joy drench my cheeks was almost like a release. Hope had finally shed a glimpse of light. Mom tightly clutched my hand as tears welled up in her eyes. "I'm so happy for you," she whispered.

It was evening by the time I got to the Hendricks'. I still had a sour taste in my mouth from being denied a pinch of Ricky's remains. But I had to let it go. Besides, I had news to share. Good news.

I stood in their majestic foyer that night, staring into the eyes of the man and woman who had created and were now grieving their beautiful son, my beloved. My heart ached for them as I wondered how they would receive what I was about to say.

"Everyone keeps telling me that I wasn't on that plane for a reason I'll probably never know," I began in a trembling voice.

Mrs. Hendrick nodded and immediately dived in. "That's right, Emily, you won't ever know."

"But, the truth is, I think I do." I paused, biting back tears, not knowing quite what to say next. "If I was on that plane, twelve people would have died." They looked confused so I quickly stammered, "I'm . . . I'm pregnant."

Mr. Hendrick started sobbing. His wife did too. I felt relieved, the news welcomed. We enjoyed a respite from the darkness that night, celebrating with smiles and hugs. They knew how worried I was, being a mom for the first time and so young. They were generous in helping me out financially from that point, which I'm so very grateful for.

I didn't stay long that night. I was exhausted and still reeling from the intense bout of morning sickness. I just wanted to go home, crawl into bed, and sleep. Without tossing and turning. Without waking up in a cold sweat wondering where Ricky was. I wanted to sleep resting in the joy of a life that was beginning to form in my belly, a life created by Ricky and me.

Sometime that weekend, Mom and I headed back to Florida. I only planned to stay for a week. At this point, my parents had sold their house on Sunset Key and taken up residence in downtown Old Town Key West. They lived in a timeless Victorian with sea-green shutters alongside other charming gingerbread-looking homes and only a block away from Duvall Street, the heartbeat of the city with its eclectic string of bars, restaurants, and shops.

I spent most of the week in bed except for frequent trips to the bathroom. I had severe bouts of morning sickness that lasted well into the afternoons. Though I didn't partake in any of the parties, I could hear it all through my open window—the laughter, the dance music and Caribbean jams, the hum of the trolley passing through at all hours. It felt strange being back in the same place where I met Ricky. So much had changed. My mind started playing tricks on me, probably given the amount of time I spent lying around, trying to sleep. I reverted to thinking that my relationship with Ricky didn't matter. That it was casual, meaningless. That I had made up our connection, our love, our promises.

And it didn't help one night, while I was getting some ginger ale and crackers from the kitchen, to be greeted by beer bottles and broken bead necklaces and some costumes I'd rather have not seen. It seemed that everyone was carrying on and having a good time. Nobody was hurting like I was. Nobody was grieving like I was. I felt if my parents truly loved me, they'd feel some of the pain I was in. Yes, they would take time to reach out and make an effort to empathize. I know Mom did her best. She was the only friend I had to lean on for support. My life was Ricky, and outside of him all I had was my mother. She made sure I was taken care of and as comfortable as I could be, even though I felt as though I was drowning in sadness, not knowing how to come up for air.

I knew I needed to refocus. To shift my perspective. To think about the baby that was beginning to form inside of me. I needed to stay strong, healthy, alive. The baby was my lifeline to Ricky. And though I knew having a child wouldn't replace his love or the person that he was, a baby would be an extension of him. Perhaps our child would share Ricky's smile. Or his twinkling eyes. Or his charm. Or the way he was so compassionate to others. Thinking of these things tempered some of my misery. It was comforting.

Feeling hopeful, I finally fell soundly asleep for the first time in two weeks. I was fired up to leave Key West and return to Charlotte to build what would be a new normal, a new life for me and one lucky little baby boy or girl.

five

There is not a parking lot in Charlotte I have not thrown up in. My morning sickness was awful and lasted for most of those glorious (insert sarcastic eye roll) nine months. But aside from puking, being aware that there was a little creature growing inside of me, an extension of the love of my life, was nothing short of awe-inspiring.

Mom came into town every now and then, and I can't tell you how much I looked forward to her visits, when we'd make pit stops in baby stores, oohing and ahhing at tiny onesies, cuddly blankets, and plush toys. Both pretty confident the baby was a boy, we even bought a blue Christmas ornament for the little guy. Though Mom and I had always been pretty tight, the baby brought us even closer.

Though I was back in the condo where Ricky and I had lived prior to the accident, I'd hang out with Ricky's parents every now and then. Mrs. Hendrick and I often reminisced about our Hawaii trip, retelling the same fun memories we made and shared only a short time before.

Though I understand there's a difference between losing a son and losing the love of your life, we were both treading the rough waters of grief. At the same time, however, I was careful not to give the Hendricks reason to worry about me.

When you go through something traumatic, there are good days and bad days. Some days you wake up and it takes every bit of strength, courage, and will to simply get out of bed and brush your teeth. Other days, armed with what I can only describe as divine, supernatural power, you feel positive, hopeful. You think, *Okay, I can make it. I can do this. Today is going to be a good day.* If the Hendricks looked like they were having one of those good days when I wasn't, I made sure not to dampen their mood. The last thing I wanted them to do was worry about how I was doing, particularly since I was carrying their grandchild.

Being pregnant was a welcome diversion. Most of the time, it helped ease the pain of loss and gave us all something to look forward to. But at times the pressure was overwhelming. I had just lost my baby's father in a tragic accident. How could I not cry? How could I not grieve? How could I not be depressed? I spent hours each day Googling the potentially harmful effects of grief on a baby in utero. This might sound crazy, but I was petrified that too much crying would hurt the baby. What if the child could feel my sadness? I could never forgive myself if somehow I hurt the little one by being too upset. After all, it was my responsibility to bring a healthy baby into the world. And I was committed to doing that.

Outside of that fear, the weight of what seemed to be a community baby gave me a sense of crushing pressure. The chaotic influx of these different emotions and thoughts weighed heavily on me. The only thing I knew to do was to withdraw, to stick by myself as much as I could. I couldn't handle anyone judging me for how I looked or how I was feeling or if I started tearing up out of the clear blue. Being alone so much did one of two things for me: either it relieved me of the pressure to act a certain way around others or it magnified my loneliness.

I couldn't not think about Ricky. I was sleeping in the bed we had shared. Watching the TV we had watched. Vacuuming the carpet we had walked on. Sitting at the table where we ate together. Reminders were everywhere. Traces of his life, our life. I'd stand in front of his closet, brushing my fingers past each shirt, closing my eyes as the scent of his cologne still lingered ever so slightly. As if he were there. As if I could take one tiny step forward and touch him, fall into his arms.

I talked to Ricky all the time. "Come back," I'd plead. "Come back to me." During many of my sleepless nights, I'd sit on the floor of my bedroom closet, turn off the light, and beg Ricky to give me a sign he was still with me. "Do something!" I'd yell with such a force my lungs felt on the verge of imploding.

I'd give Ricky options to manifest, urging him to turn on the light or throw a lamp. I wanted evidence. I wanted proof. I wanted a physical clue that his spirit was still alive, that he could still see me, that though he was gone in body, his heart was still connected to me. Somehow. Some way. I was confident, especially being pregnant, that Ricky would give me some consolation that he hadn't forgotten about me. That I wasn't alone. But lights never mysteriously switched on. Lamps were never thrown across a room. And I never saw any visions of my beloved. That was disappointing, and it fed my sense of hopelessness.

As weeks and months passed, ever so slowly, reminders of Ricky started disappearing from the condo. I came home one night after running an errand and noticed that the plans for the house we were building, his clothes, his journals, and other miscellaneous things were missing. Gone. I imagined his parents had taken them, but I didn't know for sure. And I didn't say anything for fear of anyone accusing me of being greedy, possessive, or selfish, wanting Ricky's stuff. Because that's all it was anyway. Stuff. None of it was Ricky. None of it could bring him back. I'll never forget the day his closet was finally bare. I stood staring at the empty hangers, hooks, and shelves, the white walls stark and cold. After a minute or two, I numbly shut the door. I would never open it again.

Later, as I was rummaging through some drawers in the kitchen, I found a box Ricky had kept that contained a bunch of handwritten notes and cards I had given him, as well as the matches and dinner receipt from our first date at Shula's. I was grateful for these small tokens, keepsakes that our love was real, that it existed. Around that same time Ricky's parents opened his safe and found a bunch of gifts he had been waiting to give me, including a candle I loved and a pin I had admired on a shopping excursion in Hawaii. Though I treasured these things, nothing could make me feel as connected to Ricky as the baby inside my growing belly.

I was convinced our child was a boy. I wanted it to be, so the little bugger could carry on Ricky's name. On December 15, as the technician in my obstetrician's office poured the ultrasound gel on my belly and skillfully whisked the probe around, I stared in awe at the monitor. As tiny hands and legs squirmed, I strained to see if any particular body part stood out to confirm my suspicions of a Ricky Jr. And then, "Aww, Emily. You're having a girl," the technician announced with a smile.

I sharply drew in my breath. "No, no," I whispered, shaking my head. "Can you please look again?"

She obliged, if only to humor me. After a small pause, the tech said, "Yup, trust me on this one, Emily. It's a girl, all right."

I sighed, somewhat disappointed. It wasn't that I didn't want a little girl. The baby was healthy, so who cared, right? I was just hoping for a boy so he could carry on Ricky's legacy; this was our only shot! But the letdown was short-lived. As soon as I drove home, I started dreaming of all things girly—shades of pink, textures of delicate lace, ribbons, and bows.

Naming the baby Josephine Riddick, after her daddy (who was officially Joseph Riddick), was a no-brainer. No other would do. I looked forward to June 29, my baby's arrival date, and with each passing day got a bit more swept away by envisioning the day I would finally meet and nuzzle my little one.

Though I was still sick well into my second trimester, abruptly pulling off to the sides of city highways and neighborhood streets multiple times a day so I wouldn't throw up all over my lap, I started working in the sales department at one of the Hendricks' car dealerships. I called new customers, reminding them of upcoming service appointments and maintenance that needed to be done to their newly purchased vehicles. While I was happy to swap my pajamas for some normal-people clothes and get out of the house on a daily basis, I didn't enjoy the work. It was hard for me to sound constantly chipper when I was puking up my insides every few hours. Consequently, my career in the car sales industry was short-lived. But as I was a few months away from welcoming the arrival of baby Ricki, I spent the rest of my pregnancy nesting in my new home, the house Ricky and I had lived in before we started building our dream home.

Little Ricki was growing into a big little monkey. She was close to ten pounds when her due date approached. And she was happy as could be in my womb, showing no signs of wanting to leave the warm cocoon. My doctor was worried the baby was going to get too big, so they decided to induce labor on June 29. Mr. Hendrick drove me to the hospital. I was given Pitocin, which launched me into almost immediate excruciating contractions. While I waited for an epidural, my parents, who had flown in from Florida, my brother, Ernie, Mr. and Mrs. Hendrick, and their daughter, Lynne, scattered themselves around the labor room, praying for a healthy delivery. Hours had passed, the epidural working its magic, when my doctor said it was time to push. And push I did. For close to three hours.

Pushing was useless. Ricki refused to leave my body. All that strength, energy, and sweat wasted. I had been in labor for close to twenty-four hours when I was finally wheeled into an operating room for a C-section. Mom and Mrs. Hendrick accompanied me. Physically exhausted and starving after having not eaten for close to thirty-six hours, I was strapped to a table with a curtain positioned over the front half of my body. "You're going to feel some pressure, Emily," my doctor warned, as I braced for deep pain.

As the surgery was in progress, Mrs. Hendrick peeked over the curtain, where my abdomen was being sliced open. I don't think she meant to say this out loud, but as her face turned as white as a sheet, she blurted, "Emily! They just pulled out your uterus." Good grief! The last thing I wanted to think about was my spilled organs hanging out over the outside of my body.

But then, music to my ears—a baby's cry. High pitched

and loud, baby Ricki entered a world that would never be the same. Mom squealed in delight, "Oh Emily, she's beautiful!" When the doctor lifted my baby up so I could see her, tears fell. I can't even tell you the warmth of joy I felt. Peace. Purpose. I hoped that her daddy could see her, that he could see the fullness of love he left behind.

After I'd been cleaned up, sewed up, and wheeled into the maternity ward, I was shocked to see my room full of people. Still bleary-eyed from being pumped up with morphine, body aching with pain, I quickly scanned the room, looking for baby Ricki. And there, in the swarm of a crowd that consisted of my family and the Hendricks and their friends, some of whom I didn't even recognize, was my precious bundle of joy, being passed around like a football. Everyone was over the moon, cooing over the swaddled little angel. I was happy everyone was happy, but the staggering scene stirred up fears that Ricki had, in fact, become the community baby.

She wasn't mine, I thought before gulping. She was everyone's!

I wanted everyone out so I could have a moment with the baby I had just delivered. To hold her. By myself. But I was too tired and in too much pain to speak up. So I watched the display of awe from afar, cringing as people other than her mama cradled baby Ricki.

Minutes or hours later, the crowd thinned and Ricki was whisked away to the nursery. And more minutes or hours later, a nurse popped her head in and asked if I'd like to stop by and see my baby.

Yes please!

I bawled when I sat in the padded rocking chair in the

nursery holding my girl. It wasn't just maternal ecstasy that fueled the tears; it was also the weight of responsibility I imagine most young mothers feel. *Good golly. This is it. The day I've been waiting for. I have a baby. I'm actually a mom.* And then, a wave of slight panic. *Well, now what? What am I supposed to do? What do I need to do? Where is the baby manual? Who's going to give me instructions? Where's my FAQ sheet?*

As I rocked back and forth, nestling little Ricki up to my face, staring into her eyes, a mirror of her daddy's eyes, I felt soothing peace. Oh, the fears were still there, but in the midst were pride and joy and calm. I touched Ricki's delicate skin, soft and pink. Every feature perfect. My baby. Ricky's baby. Then, the rush of tears.

I was in the hospital for about three days. I suffered from a severe bout of anemia, and almost depleted of iron, I could barely stand up, let alone move. When the doctor told me I was finally healthy enough to go home, I would have jumped up and down for joy if not for the stitches stapled in my tummy.

Mom and Dad stayed with me for a few days while I stumbled through fatigue like a typical new mom in a haze of changing diapers, frequent feedings, and moments I'd stare at Ricki, marveling at this beautiful new creature who had created within me a whole new world.

I remember waking up during those first few days at home after a much-needed power nap to a house full of people. Though I did appreciate all the help my parents and the Hendricks gave me during that time, I was disappointed that I had what felt like only a few moments alone with my daughter. The bonding time I desperately craved and deserved seemed cut short by others hovering over her. Overcome by exhaustion and overwhelmed by the lack of personal space, I know I had moments when my frayed nerves got the best of me.

After my parents left, I enlisted the help of a woman named Margarita, a sweetheart from Colombia who didn't speak much English. Even though there was a gap in communication, she was a godsend, spending a few hours a day with Ricki and me, loving on the baby and helping me heal and care for her.

As weeks passed into months, Ricki's personality started to develop and shine. She was a happy baby with the sweetest temperament and more rolls on her chunky body than you would find in a bakery. She always smiled, gurgled, and cooed. And when she laughed, oh my goodness, I'd just about bust out laughing every time I heard those deep-bellied squeals of delight. I strolled her around the park, pushing her on the swings as she howled with laughter. I took her to the movies with me, watching the film as she'd cuddle up and fall asleep on my chest. I took her for crazy rides up and down the aisles during our grocery shopping excursions. I took her to Mommy and Me classes around the neighborhood and watched her interact with other kids her age as they bounced, tumbled, sang, and danced as only little ones can do.

When Ricki turned one, I threw her an intimate birthday party at my house with family and a few friends, wondering, like most parents do, where on earth the time went. My little girl took her first step around that time. Mr. Hendrick and I were on the bus at a race. Watching him eat a slice of cheesy pizza, Ricki held out her hand for a bite and then took a step toward him to make the effort to get it herself. Mr. Hendrick and I stared at each other for a second, then started laughing. "Is that official?" he chuckled. It sure was!

Little Ricki was an anchor, a blessing in the middle of the fog that shrouded me still, more than a year after she was born. Though I was never diagnosed officially, looking back, I can see now that I suffered from postpartum depression. I hadn't fully grieved the loss of my baby girl's dad because I was so scared that a burst of spontaneous tears or deep reflection about the loss would somehow harm the baby. And once Ricki was born, well, I had to take care of her. I didn't have time to healthily process the pain, the loss that got squashed down deeper and deeper in the midst of responsibility.

I felt alone. I had little Ricki and I was grateful for her. No doubt she was a gift, a blessing. But I was lonely. Lost. Desperate. Girls my age were in college, deciding on majors, planning for their futures. They were spending Friday nights and weekends at the movies or hanging out at parties or going on hot dates or shopping for cute clothes or studying for exams and concerning themselves with what they were going to do when they grew up. I felt unsettled. I didn't know what I wanted or what I wanted to do with my life other than take care of my daughter. I was struggling as a new mom and didn't have anyone my age to talk to about it.

I longed for attention. I had little to no self-respect, and I had so much pent-up grief that needed an outlet, a healthy one, so I wouldn't come undone. You'd think I'd turn to God, but I didn't. Maybe I wasn't ready. Or I just didn't know how. Besides, I wanted personal companionship, real-life people I could talk to and do fun things with. Not knowing where to turn, I started hanging out with a fast crowd that liked to have a good time. And in the process of trying to divert attention away from feeling empty, I made some foolish decisions, ones I am not proud of.

I was also still trying to decide what I wanted to do. I thought about opening a boutique or giving fashion a whirl. I didn't know. Speed Channel reached out to me sometime in 2006 to host *Three Wide Life*, a TV show about the lives of race-car drivers off the track. It was fun and I was grateful for the opportunity. But after doing a few episodes and having to memorize pages and pages of scripts, I realized it wasn't a great fit. Life as a single mom resumed its course. I spent most of my days with Ricki and visited regularly with the Hendricks so they could get to know their precious granddaughter. Ever since she was a baby and also as she got older, I would show Ricki pictures of her daddy and always made sure she knew how much he loved her. I know the Hendricks did the same.

When Ricki was around two, I continued to plod along in a funk. I was floating, trying to piece together a life without any solid direction. A friend of mine lived in Nashville, and I thought it'd be great to spend New Year's there. I wanted to get away, find some space outside of Charlotte, outside of the days that seemed to weave right into the next without much distinction.

I loved everything about Nashville. The music (it was everywhere, and not just country!), the people (good old Southern charm and hospitality), the artsy vibe (the neighborhood where my friend lived was full of hipsters)—most of all I loved the anonymity. Though Charlotte is far from a small town, the fact that the accident occurred within the NASCAR family made such huge headlines, sometimes it felt like there was this blinding spotlight on me, especially after giving birth to Ricki. In Nashville, nobody knew me. And frankly nobody cared. I didn't feel the pressure, as I did in Charlotte, to act a certain way to fulfill grieving-widow protocol or standards, not that I even knew what that meant.

As I flew back to North Carolina, I knew I wanted to move to Nashville. I needed a change, a fresh start. Maybe the move would clarify some direction, help me sort out who I was, what I wanted to do. Outside of giving birth to Ricki, it was the first thing that I had gotten excited about in a long time. Unfortunately, not everyone shared my enthusiasm.

Things between the Hendricks and me were pretty tense at the time. They didn't want Ricki away from them. And though I respected and appreciated all they'd done for us, I was in my early twenties and a mom, for Pete's sake. I had to make some decisions on my own. Unfortunately, my own mother also disagreed with my decision. "Don't do it," she warned, mentioning something to the effect that I wouldn't be able to run away from myself. Her response was disappointing. Nobody could understand how I was still reeling from the overwhelming chain of events that had transformed me from a giddy and relatively carefree youngster-in-love to tragically losing the love of my life, nursing a pregnancy, and becoming a single mom at the age of nineteen.

I wanted to breathe. I needed space. I wanted to stop crying myself to sleep each night and having to put on a happy face as soon as my alarm sounded so I could watch *Sesame Street* and play dolls with Ricki without her wondering what was wrong with Mama. Something had to give.

And so I took a calculated risk and moved to Nashville, where I spent two years and learned a lot about myself. For starters, I wasn't a total waste of a human being. I was on my own. Though Dad helped support Ricki and me, I took an eight-dollar-an-hour retail job and lived simply, giving to my daughter just the basics like food and clothes and indulging in occasional fun outings at Gymboree-type places. We went without the excess we were both used to back in Charlotte. Also, being together in a new world bonded us. I felt I finally had her to myself.

Now don't get me wrong. I know it takes a village to raise a child, and I can't say thank you enough to my parents, the Hendricks, and others who pitched in and helped. But there was something so different, special, and intimate when life was just about Ricki and me. I fell in love with her all over again. We went to the park almost every day. It was awesome to watch Ricki attack the playground, sailing down the slides, whipping around the monkey bars like a pro. She was fearless and adventurous, just like her daddy. At night, we'd curl up in my bed. I'd read through a stack of bedtime stories until her eyes got heavy. Though she had her own room, Ricki would often fall asleep in mine. I didn't enjoy being accidently kicked in random places throughout the night, but snuggling with her was the best. I savored those moments, brushing her blonde locks with my fingers as she drifted off to sleep. Knowing she was right beside me brought comfort. It made missing Ricky just a little bit more bearable.

I often took Ricki down to the pool in our apartment complex where I started chatting up a girl around my age named (of all names) Emily. She introduced me to other girls who I immediately clicked with and who liked me for me. Plain ol' Emily Maynard. I wasn't big-bucks Emily, or special-connections Emily, or please-get-me-tickets-to-NASCAR Emily. I liked being regular Emily.

My friend Emily, a successful and very driven real-estate agent, encouraged me to think about becoming a real-estate agent. I laughed. At least at first. But then I figured, why not? I signed up for a two-week class, frying my brain with legal terms and pulling many all-nighters studying.

Plugging through the course took every ounce of energy, but I did it. I got my real-estate license as well as a job with a local agency named French, Christianson, Patterson. This stint didn't last long. The economy was in a slump and I ended up showing houses to creepy guys who wanted to discuss sales "over dinner" or "over a drink."

Times got tough. I realized Mom, as always, was right. I could have moved anywhere. I could have planted myself in Paris or Manhattan or California, and ultimately my situation would have stayed the same. I would carry with me that same emptiness I'd been trying so hard to avoid, ignore, or fill with meaningless things. I couldn't replace that vacuum in my soul with anything. Ricky wasn't coming back. A successful career wouldn't plug it up. Fun outings with friends and even cute guys wouldn't make a difference. My heart was longing for an identity. Not in things or people but in Christ. I'd learn this later.

When I moved to Nashville, I went to church regularly and started praying more often. Sure, a lot of them were of the please-help-me variety, but the point is I maintained an open line of communication with God. I felt drawn to Him, still, in light of some bad choices I had made since Ricky had passed away. The pull I felt toward God was so strong, but I didn't dive deep, though I wish I had. That's probably my biggest regret—I truly believe that a deeper relationship with Him would have kept me from making the wrong decisions, or at least made me pause long enough to question what I was doing and why.

I prayed to find relief from the ache in my heart. I missed Ricky something fierce. Sometimes I'd wonder if he was mad at me or if he even liked the person I'd become. Other times, I'd dream about what life would look like if he were still with me. We'd be married, of course, living in Charlotte, having had or on our way to having baby number two. Ricki was starting to notice when I was sad.

I'll never forget putting up Christmas decorations one year. Though the holidays were always tough and the last thing I wanted to do was belt out some fa-la-las and be jolly, I was determined to make the season as magical as I could for my daughter. That was the least she deserved. So that year I had bought a cute little tree as tall as my daughter, a stack of web tutorials (this was prior to Pinterest, can you believe it?), and a box of festive decorations that I, with confidence, precision, and skill, prepared to artfully adorn on the aromatic pine sapling. I started this festive project by wrapping beaded garland and sparking lights around the tree. It only took a few revolutions before I ended up with a tangled web of snarled and knotted wires. Trying to unscramble the mess proved pointless.

I got so frustrated, I turned into the Hulk, ripping the garland apart and helplessly watching beads fly every which way, falling to the floor like pellets from a BB gun. And the lights? A few choice words and many broken bulbs later, they found a new home in the trash can. Well, eventually, after sitting in a pathetic, mangled heap in a corner after being thrown there. Sobbing, I sat on the floor scattered with a layer of sharp needles and lone beads.

Ricki was in the other room and came running when the commotion broke out. She looked at me sympathetically, placed her chubby little-girl hand in mine, and said with compassionate insight well beyond her years, "Mommy, you miss Daddy, don't you?"

"Yes, Ricki," I sighed. "I sure do."

And I always will.

I grew up a lot in Nashville. I appreciated my independence, the bonds I formed with neat friends, and the realizations I made that change wasn't about geography—that the same problems, the same painful realities, the same inner conflicts I wrestled with would stay with me wherever I went. Moving back to Charlotte wasn't a bad idea. I knew Ricki missed her grandparents. And though I had made some good friends, I wasn't married to the idea of staying.

A month or so later, I drove east on Interstate 40, heading back to North Carolina with four-year-old Ricki sleeping soundly, surrounded by two years' worth of stuff spilling out of boxes. I had carefully placed Ricki's new pet, a shiny goldfish, in a glass bowl between my legs, careful not to prompt any spillage. As I drove into the early morning, just as the sun was making its grand appearance, tears fell. I clutched the steering wheel with trembling hands as the waterworks gushed. The ugly-cry kind. Oh sure, I was ready to return to Charlotte, but I was going to miss the home, my own space, I had created in Nashville. I called my friend Emily and others on the way, reminding them how much I appreciated them and how much I was going to miss them.

Wally Lamb wrote, "The seeker embarks on a journey to find what he wants and discovers, along the way, what he needs."[*] A seeker. That was me. I had taken some risks. Tried new things. Opened my heart to friendships. Stumbled at times, eventually regaining my balance. And learned. I still didn't know what I was going to do with my life, but I was beginning to discover who I was. Baby steps. Microscopic, but progress nonetheless.

---

[*] Wally Lamb, *The Hour I First Believed* (New York: Harper Luxe, 2008), 697.

six

G uess what, Emily?" my friend Nikki, who I had met on my eighteenth birthday, asked with a sheepish smile as she sat at my kitchen table watching me put away groceries. Not really waiting for me to respond, she quickly burst out, "I nominated you for *The Bachelor*."

As my jaw dropped, so did the carton of eggs I was trying to balance while shoving a gallon of milk into the fridge. "What are you talking about?" I demanded, annoyed that I had to clean up a million tiny pieces of shattered eggshells and puddles of slimy yolk. *The Bachelor*? I knew the show well, of course. It was a guilty pleasure I watched regularly, usually tuning in with my girlfriends, wine glasses in hand. We'd take turns making jabs at the contestants on the show.

The whole setup seemed kinda weird. Why on earth would any self-respecting woman desperately vie for some schmuck's attention and affection on national TV with twenty-some other women doing the same with the same guy? Though the show was fantastically entertaining, the concept was too unorthodox for my taste. Thanks, but no thanks, Nikki. I'd had enough drama in my life, and I liked the current temperature, settled and calm. Well, at least that's where my head was at that time.

I'd been back in Charlotte for a few months and just started a job as an event coordinator for the Levine Children's Hospital. I was in charge of managing fund-raisers, selling tables for galas, and organizing awareness initiatives for the pediatric intensive care centers. I loved working for this organization, especially being able to help others.

Overall, I was in a great place. I was happy to be back in North Carolina. The transition was pretty seamless, confirming I had made the right decision. My twenty-four-year-old self had a wonderful group of friends, was going to church, and was overall enjoying life. Five-year-old Ricki was having the time of her life in kindergarten and being close once again to her grandparents.

Granted, I was lonely. At times I'd feel the ache of not having a companion, a special someone to do life with my little girl and me. I tried not to think about it that much, but whenever I'd hear of someone I knew getting engaged or married, a dash of disappointment would sprinkle right on top of my heartfelt congratulations.

Apparently, I was more dissatisfied with my single status than I thought. Nikki, who knew me inside and out, was brutally honest with me that day. "Emily, I love you. But I'm tired of hearing you complain about being single," she admitted, though still being her sweet Southern self. "Look, I had to do something." I didn't get how throwing me to the wolves on national TV would be considered an appropriate "something."

My reservation aside, the whole thing was pretty funny. While the idea of being considered as a contestant on *The*

Bachelor was ridiculous, what I thought was more ridiculous was actually getting picked out of thousands of girls. There was no way I'd get chosen. Nikki went on her way, and as I spent the next few days continuing to do typical, everyday mom stuff, like driving Ricki to and from school, working, doing laundry, and cleaning, I forgot all about her announcement.

One day the phone rang. The man on the other line said he was a casting director for *The Bachelor*. Not taking his introduction seriously, I snickered and said, "I'm not interested, sir," before he continued.

I repeated my thanks but no thanks, but before I could hang up, the man said, "Just give me one more minute, Emily. Your friend Nikki, she wrote and told us all about you. Just give me a few more seconds so I can read to you what she had to say." Once he mentioned Nikki, I finally realized this wasn't a prank call. And I ended up staying on the line, but only because I was curious about what Nikki had written in her letter.

As the casting director read a beautifully written letter, in it some of the nicest words that anyone had ever said about me, I started crying. Nikki's kind thoughts just about blew me away. My emotions got the best of me and the few tears turned into an all-out I-can't-get-a-word-out crying. I could just imagine this man beaming from ear to ear, thinking, *Good grief, this woman's in tears already? She's a shoo-in!* Though I appreciated Nikki's complimentary thoughts and was shocked and very flattered that I was even being considered to be on *The Bachelor*, I still didn't want to be on the show. And I told that to the casting director.

But the guy kept calling—and e-mailing. And calling—and e-mailing. He finally convinced me to fly out to Los Angeles for a weekend just to learn more about the opportunity and to get a feel for the process. No strings. Nothing to lose. I was intrigued and agreed, making arrangements for my mom, who wasn't jumping for joy at my decision, to fly into town so she could spend a few days with Ricki while I was gone.

When I arrived at LAX less than two weeks after that first phone call, I was picked up by a town car and shuttled to a non-descript hotel. The whole scene was very hush-hush. No one had given me an itinerary or a plan. I didn't have a clue what was going on. I was assigned a handler from the show whose job was to shuffle me back and forth to different conference rooms around the hotel that weekend. Outside of navigating my way through a maze of hallways escorted by a handler, I had to remain alone in my room. I couldn't even walk down to the lobby to get a Diet Coke or a bag of chips.

That afternoon, I had my first interview. Keep in mind I still wasn't sold on the idea. My only intention up to this point was to gather information. That's it. What I didn't know, how-ever, was that the producers had their own agenda. Rather than simply arm me with the lowdown of the show, they wanted to check me out to see if my personality meshed well and to ensure I wasn't a total whack job (the serial-killer kind, not the good kind of nut that makes for entertaining TV).

Before my first interview, I was given a packet of papers to sign and a two-inch-thick detailed personality questionnaire to fill out. Finally, I walked into an empty and dimly lit, almost-pitch-black room. A producer began interrogating me with a bunch of questions about my personal life while a cameraman filmed the process.

"Has anyone taken any pictures of you?"

"Oh sure," I said, before I realized he was talking about the provocative, birthday-suit kind, not the here-are-Ricki-and-me-at-Chuck-E-Cheese kind.

More questions followed. What did I like about the show? How would I describe my personality? The questions kept coming, random ones. No topic was off-limits. It was exhausting. When the interview was over, I was escorted out. Thinking I was going to be taken down another hallway and ultimately back to my room, I started dreaming about the lovely nap I planned to take to give my brain a rest.

No such luck.

I was shown into another room, brighter with windows. A big-screen TV monitor was positioned at the front where the interview yours truly had just finished a minute ago was being played. About twenty people, who I later learned were producers, sat in chairs organized in a semicircle watching me answer some question or other. I was mortified. To say the least, it's uncomfortable to watch yourself on screen while all eyes are on you. I was confused and turned to the handler, hoping she could give me at least a clue of what was going on. But she just directed me to an empty chair right in the middle of the circle and in front of the TV screen. One of the producers paused the interview from a remote and the interrogation was under way.

"So, Emily, who's your favorite guy from this season of *The Bachelorette*?" someone called out. Season 6 with Ali Fedotowsky was currently airing, and though I had watched a few episodes, no guy stood out. Certainly no one I would leave home for two months for. No offense, but none of them was my type. I thought I needed someone older, refined, sophisticated. Heck, what did I know?

"None, to be honest," I replied.

"What about any other season?" another producer asked, then added, "We just want to get a feel for who your type is, Emily."

I thought for a moment and said, "Brad Womack." I know. I'd just offered the name of, at the time, the most hated Bachelor of the entire show. A bit loony, don't you think?

I noticed two producers immediately look at each other, both making a funny face. I imagined they thought he was an odd pick. After all, nobody liked Brad. And perhaps for good reason.

"Tell us what you like about Brad," someone else asked.

"He's manly, Southern, rugged," I answered. "And I feel bad for him because he got such a terrible backlash for his decision." It sounds odd now, but I actually liked the fact that Brad didn't pick anyone. And I did think he was a nice guy who didn't get a fair shake. Never in a million years did I imagine he'd actually be on the show. The thought never even crossed my mind.

Then, more questions.

"Why are you still single?"

"What do you like in a guy?"

"What don't you like in a guy?"

When the questions stopped coming, I had a final interview with a private investigator and was given a thorough background check. Then, the end of the two-day adventure. A producer shook my hand and said, "Thank you, Emily. That's it for now. We'll be in touch."

On the plane heading back to Charlotte, I eased into my seat, thinking about what had just transpired. It was an unusual two days—that was for sure. I didn't know what the next step was. More waiting, I supposed. I didn't have this overwhelming sense of "Oh my goodness! I definitely want to be on the show," but I also wasn't totally opposed to the idea, as I had been at first. I also wondered how Ricki would fit into the picture, my biggest concern, and what my parents would think if by some strange collision of fate and chance I actually ended up on *The Bachelor*. Thankfully, before I had the chance to worry away the next few hours, I dozed off.

A few days later I received an e-mail from the show. "Congratulations, Emily. You've been chosen to be on season 15 of *The Bachelor*." Wow! Talk about a surreal moment! But I hadn't yet made a decision. I let the e-mail sit for days, unanswered. Then came the barrage of phone calls from producers. My mind spun in nauseating circles. This was all happening too fast for my comfort. By the time I got the guts to call someone back, I repeated my previous response of thanks but no thanks. I wasn't comfortable enough to say yes, and besides, no one, other than Nikki, seemed to think it was a good idea.

When Mom and I had a heart-to-heart about the opportunity, she wasn't as excited about the opportunity as I would have liked. She had recently watched an episode of *The Bachelor Pad*, and under no circumstances would she support her daughter partying, carrying on, and disrespecting herself on national TV. "Please, Emily. Don't do it," Mom begged. "They're going to eat you alive." She was being protective, a natural instinct for any mother. Who "they" were, I didn't know. The other girls? The media? The American public? All the above?

When a producer called one night trying to convince me to do the show, I purged all my fears on him. "How could I leave Ricki? What if I get portrayed terribly? And is the whole show even real? It doesn't have a positive track record!"

"I'll tell you what, Emily," the producer said. "Just say yes and come meet the guy."

I replied, "But say I think the guy is a total jerk or just not for me. Then you'll probably work your editing magic and make me out to be some lunatic."

He laughed. "I promise you, Emily, we won't. But I also promise you, you're gonna like the guy." Something in his voice seemed reassuring.

And so, a week before filming, the end of October 2010, I finally agreed to do the show. At the tail end of the nonstop worrying, pondering, and questioning lay two big words: *Why not?* Maybe, just maybe—and I'm telling you at the time I was convinced of this—God planned for me to meet my husband this way. True, it was unconventional. And a little strange. But my life had been pretty unusual up to this point, so what was the difference? Though Mom was disappointed, she was quick to get on board and agreed to watch Ricki for me. I didn't know exactly how long I'd be gone, but Mom graciously blocked out her schedule for the full two months, just in case.

My yes required signing my life away, so it seemed, in a contract thicker than my real-estate textbooks. I was sworn to secrecy starting the moment my signature was on the page until a certain time well after the show would air. I was not to have contact with the outside world during filming, which meant no phone calls to anyone—not family, friends, or media—and no access to the Internet or e-mail. I couldn't share details about the show or the filming process with anyone. I was basically enclosed in a bubble for the next few months. ABC was very accommodating, however, considering my single-mom status and my earlier hesitance to do the show. The network made allowances for me to call and check in with Ricki on a daily basis. I wouldn't have done the show without that exception, so thank you again, ABC!

The contract was accompanied by a vague packing list. The list was so ambiguous I needed help—and fast.

I enlisted the keen eyes of my fashionista buddies and turned my guest bedroom into a packing room. While Ricki slept, Nikki and others leaned over a bed covered in what seemed like thousands of articles of clothing—from bathing suits to T-shirts to cocktail dresses. My gal pals helped me create a two-month wardrobe, matching weather-appropriate tops and bottoms and organizing them into daywear and nightwear, taking pictures of every outfit so I could remember what pieces went with what. There was no way I was going to get through filming and freak out because I didn't have a thing to wear. My friends were awesome!

There was only one teeny hitch. The dress we had painstakingly chosen for the first rose ceremony needed alterations. We spent a lot of time and thought making the decision because if I got sent home that first night—which I prayed I wouldn't; nobody wants to be that girl—I wanted to at least look good while getting rejected. I dropped the dress off at a local tailor, feeling confident that a few days was plenty of time to get it fixed before I flew out to Los Angeles.

Though I was heartbroken at leaving Ricki for so long, I knew she was in good hands. She loved her Mimi (what she called her grandmother) and was thrilled to get to spend so much time with her. Because *The Bachelor* is a very complicated concept for a five-year-old to understand, I told Ricki that I was working, hosting a special show, but that I'd call her every single day to tell her I loved her. I left Ricki presents for each day I'd be gone, as many days as the best-case scenario of making it to the final rose ceremony. In secret places, I hid a bunch of Barbies, coloring books, and other toys attached with notes telling her how much I missed and loved her.

While Ricki got gifts, my mom wasn't so lucky. She got the boring stuff, like a ten-page instruction list of how to care for her granddaughter, complete with a list of Ricki's favorite foods, a detailed hour-by-hour schedule, and every emergency contact number, from our pediatrician to the local police department. Mom never looked at the meticulously prepared booklet. She shoved it right back in my face, rolling her eyes. "Emily, this is insulting. I've raised two kids. I know what I'm doing."

Point taken. It's not that I underestimated my mother. I was just nervous leaving my daughter for too long.

The day before I left for Los Angeles, I picked up the dress I had dropped off earlier for some alterations. When I tried it on, I was horrified to find out nothing had been done. It had the same unflattering potato-sack shape. "You have to fix it!" I shrieked at the tailor, fully aware that my flight was in less than twenty hours. After profuse apologies, the woman promised it'd be ready first thing the next day. I'd have to pick it up on my way to the airport.

I woke up the next morning with a lump in my throat and a knot in my stomach. Nerves. Sadness. I already missed Ricki and I hadn't even left yet. *What am I doing?* I wondered as I stared at my two giant suitcases and checked my flight status on my phone, the last time I'd be able to use it for a while.

On time.

This was one occasion I wouldn't have minded seeing the word Delayed.

The car ride to the airport was a tear fest. After picking up the dress, Mom drove, and Ricki and I nestled as close to each other as we could in the back, our seat belts crushing us. I cried. Ricki cried. And when Mom noticed our tears when she glanced in the rearview mirror, her own started trickling down her cheeks. I knew Ricki would be okay, but the dismal thought of us being apart for so long started chipping away at the golden façade of this opportunity. I also knew I was going to miss my mother. Over the past few years, she had become my best friend.

Standing outside the terminal in the orbit of passenger arrivals, where some good-byes were brief and others lingered, I pulled my little girl closer into my chest, smelling her freshly washed hair. I think the good-bye was hardest on me. Ricki, just like her dad, was an adaptable kid. She handled change well, never coming unhinged when her routine got interrupted. I, however, was a blubbering mess of sobs and forced smiles, doing my best, obviously unsuccessfully, to put on a brave front, saying good-bye to my two favorite people in the world.

"Move it, ladies," an annoyed-looking policeman barked in my direction, before sounding his whistle.

"I'll call you when I land," I promised Ricki, who grabbed my face in her chubby little-girl hands and beamed, "I love you, Mommy." And off she pranced, holding on to her beloved Mimi's hand as she climbed into the backseat. I stood on the sidewalk, waving at the two of them until the taillights of the car were unrecognizable specks.

Ready or not, *Bachelor*, here I come.

"We have to send for an SUV," the driver said, annoyed, as his gaze shifted from me to my two trunks of luggage. That's right, I said *trunks*. One was so big, it could have been used as a furniture piece.

I was only allowed to bring two suitcases. Although I'm a stickler for rules, there was no way I was going to fit a two-month wardrobe of hot-weather and cold-weather clothes, loungewear, swimwear, formal dresses, jewelry, accessories, heels, boots, flip-flops, and a bathroom of toiletries, which probably demanded its own suitcase, in two regular-sized airport bags. Let's be realistic.

Since downsizing my wardrobe wasn't an option, I had no choice but to upsize my luggage. Problem was, the trunks I used didn't fit into the town car the show had sent to pick me up from the airport. And when the driver told me they'd have to send for another car, a bigger one, well, I was certainly not going to be *that* girl. I didn't want to set off the high-maintenance panic alarm before I even arrived at the Bachelor mansion. Petrified at this thought, I told the driver, "Look, I'll do whatever I need to do to make these things fit." I meant it.

For the next fifteen minutes, we pushed and pulled and turned and shoved and repositioned and readjusted, and finally, with sweat pouring through my blouse, we drove off, me sitting in the front passenger seat uncomfortably lodged alongside a gigantic piece of luggage. Though our efforts were successful, the driver still looked sour. I sighed. I wasn't getting off to a very good start. I wondered if he was going to go to the producers and complain about what a diva I was.

Desperate not to come off as a prima donna, I tried to butter the guy up with small talk.

"Boy, the traffic is pretty bad," I remarked as we sat in bumper-to-bumper traffic on a smog-filled highway.

"Well, this is L.A.," he replied curtly, immediately turning up the radio and drowning out my feeble attempts at chitchat.

I resigned myself to staring out the window on the way to the hotel. Without conversation, my mind raced. *Wait. What is happening? Is this for real? Oh my goodness. I'm a contestant on* The Bachelor. *What in the world?*

My mind flitted from one thought to the next. *What if the girls don't like me? What if I don't like the guy? What if I get sent home the first night? What if I trip and face plant on camera? What if my words get twisted and I'm portrayed as the awful spoiled-brat girl? What if—oh dear Lord—what if I actually meet the man I'm going to marry?*

As we pulled into a Radisson hotel, a handler from the show hurried out and accompanied me to my room and spouted off a loose schedule. The next day and a half would consist of interviews, when I would be asked a hundred different versions of "How are you doing / feeling?" followed by a photo shoot for my ABC bio, and then—nobody told me this part—hours of downtime, waiting, alone in my hotel room. I wasn't allowed to talk to anyone, let alone meet any of the other girls.

The day before the famous limousine ride to the Bachelor mansion, the show's fabulous stylist, who is so intimidating merely because of how amazing he is, bounced into my room to check out the dress I planned to wear on that first night, the one I'd picked up on my way to the airport. As he held up my choice, slowly eyeing it up and down, side to side, I hoped he wouldn't toss it into a corner with contempt. Thankfully, the stylist gave the thumbs-up. I was relieved, but after he left, as I eyed the dress in the same manner he had, I noticed it looked small. Really small. Like could-practically-fit-my-daughter small.

The next morning, I was told to get ready, though I wouldn't be arriving at the mansion until later that night. A makeup artist and hairstylist came by to doll me up, the only time I'd have these amazing men and women work their magic. When the room emptied and I started pulling on my dress, I heard a knock at the door. "Sound guy!" someone belted from the hall. "I'm here to mic you up."

"One minute!" I yelled, frantically trying to pull up the dress that was, in fact, so tight I was terrified the seams were going to pop. Another knock sounded as I finally wrangled the beautiful black number up and over my back, zipping it with relief. I was happy I got it on, not so much that it was like a second layer of skin and I could barely breathe. When the soundman came in and I saw the mic pack in his hand, I groaned. Somehow, by the grace of God, that two-inch-thick transmitter had to shimmy its way down my back underneath the suffocating fabric. And somehow, by that same grace of God and a considerable amount of inhaling, sucking in, twisting, and turning, I zipped that dress back up, mic'd and ready to go. Granted, the dress was choking the living daylights out of my ribs and pushing up my lady parts to my chin, but by golly, I did it. I prayed all night that the zipper wouldn't pop off and take someone's eye out.

It was nine in the evening by the time I was taken to the hotel lobby to meet the five other girls with whom I'd be sharing the limo ride to meet the Bachelor. Lisa M., a sweet girl from Kansas, was there, along with two other women who I'm afraid I don't remember because they were sent home later that night. Keltie Colleen, a leggy former Rockette, and drop-dead gorgeous Michelle Money were also in the mix, chatting away like besties. I was struck by how confident they looked and acted, and in my insecurity I shyly retreated into my shell.

I don't remember saying much more than a "Hi, how are you?" to the group before the producer assigned to us shuffled us to the waiting limo. I do remember asking Keltie a question and her looking at me befuddled, as if I had just spoken to her in Cantonese. She turned to Michelle and asked, "What did Emily just say?" Apparently, my Southern accent made my words unintelligible—as well as fodder for an awkward moment. Though later the three of us, as well as Lisa, would become close, I didn't feel a connection with them on the limo ride. Then again, it was hard to feel much of anything while being so overwhelmed with anxiety.

All our belongings were packed in our suitcases and manned by a crew member. Whoever would be going home later that night would find her bags by the front door as she was leaving the house for good. Our bags would be packed every rose ceremony going forward, so whoever was sent home had no time to say good-bye to the other girls once the Bachelor said good-bye to her.

The ride to the house, more so the super painfully slow climb to the top of the driveway, where our male prize awaited our arrival, seemed to take forever. Sometimes we waited in the limo; other times we were told to get out, stand around, and wait for makeup artists to scurry around and touch up our hair and faces. Then we were herded back into the limo and told to wait some more. I listened quietly while the girls tossed ideas around of who the Bachelor would be. None of us knew for sure.

When we finally stopped in front of the house, Michelle blurted, "It's Brad Womack!"

I started shaking. I whipped around to face the window and see if it was true. By golly, there he was. Brad. Well, I'll be darned. I grabbed the producer's hand and said, "Oh my gosh, this is crazy!"

He smiled and said, "We told you you'd like him." All the girls were anxious to meet the dreamboat, giggling and primping. I felt like I was going to throw up.

Keltie shimmied out of the limo first, showing off her limber dance skills with a high kick. Michelle was next, sauntering up to Brad and reeking of sex appeal. As the other girls got out one by one, I sat frozen, trying to scrounge up ideas to make for a memorable entrance. *Okay, I can't dance, let alone kick. And I'm not sexy. I can't sing or compose a haiku on the spot. What the heck am I going to say or do?* Earlier, a producer had asked me to think about what I'd like to do or say at my first rendezvous with the Bachelor.

I hated the thought of a contrived introduction. Whenever I had watched the show in the past, I would make fun of anyone for spouting off a cheesy one-liner that had obviously been planned out well in advance. I thought I'd rely on spontaneity, refusing to put on a show, giggle and feel his muscles, or say something corny. But while sitting and waiting for my cue to get out of the limo and start walking toward Brad, I could have kicked myself in the behind—if my dress wasn't so tight— for not coming up with something witty. Or just something, period. *Oh crap*, is what I thought as I opened the car door and tried as gracefully as I could to exit the limo.

When you watch the show at home and see the trail of girls making this famous trek to meet who they hope is the man of their dreams, you hear music, background music in sync with each careful, stilettoed step. But when you do it in real life, outside of masterful editing, all you hear is crickets. It's awkward, people. Really awkward.

Brad was as tall and as dreamy as I had seen him on TV. I couldn't stop smiling and I didn't know what to say except, "I'm so excited to be here" and, "I'm so glad it's you." I repeated these things about five times during the course of our few-minute conversation. Then I scurried off like a nervous mouse.

I don't know what was more nerve-wracking—meeting Brad for the first time or what happened immediately afterward, walking into a living room full of the competition, the twenty-nine other girls, showing off their perfectly coifed hair, fit bodies, and smoky eyes.

I didn't know whether to sit or stand or drink or not drink the champagne in my hand. I set about looking for some producers I knew, familiar faces. Aside from being the movers and shakers of making the show a hit, they are also nice people, many I still keep in touch with, which is why, during this cocktail gathering, I wanted so desperately to hang out and talk to one of them. But I couldn't find anyone I recognized.

Everywhere I turned, all the bachelorettes were talking about how Chantal slapped Brad. I kept quiet, keeping a low profile and listening to the conversations. I didn't say much of anything to anyone and for that reason probably came off as either standoffish or creepy. (Later, some of the women would tell me they couldn't believe how shy I was that first night!) I was so on the fringe of the intense social dynamic, that when I overheard a producer ask a bunch of girls, me included, to talk about "the vampire," my first thought was, *Who?* I hadn't even noticed the beautiful blonde with fangs!

As introverted as I appeared, I was still stoked about getting to meet Brad. But so were twenty-nine other women. Women who returned from their vis-à-vis all saying different versions of the same thing: "Brad is so awesome! We had such a connection!" I sipped on champagne in the background, flashing back to my encounter with Brad. All I knew was that it wasn't an epic failure.

Most of that first night was an exhausting blur. By the time Brad was done meeting and mingling with his harem, it was about two in the morning. My energy tank was waning. Outside of saying our initial hello, I hadn't had any one-on-one time with Brad but was content to just wait around and see what happened. Sitting on the couch, listening to the noisy and nonstop chatter and giggles, I started nodding off when a producer grabbed me by the arm and told me to follow him to the back of the house. "Brad wants to see you," he whispered.

Someone directed me to an outdoor bench littered with red throw pillows. Lit candles (the most favored *Bachelor* and *Bachelorette* prop) rested on every inch of tabletop space available. A cameraman positioned himself to my side as I waited. Yawn. And waited some more. Waiting can be an enemy. It gave me space to do some mental gymnastics. *How's my posture? Do I look like a hunchback? Why is Brad taking so long? Maybe he just found the love of his life and decided to send everyone home.*

Once I heard footsteps, I started full-fledge panicking. What would I say? What should I say? I figured I'd act as I would on a normal date. You know, one without me needing to wear a mic pack or being accompanied by producers and cameramen. I wouldn't bring or memorize talking points while chatting up a suitor over coffee, so being myself and letting the conversation flow organically seemed the best option. And if that meant a quiet or awkward conversation, so be it.

Brad was a gentleman, sweet and kind. He listened intently and was very down to earth. I liked that. I could tell he was nervous, which made me feel better. But while he put me at ease, my nerves were still wobbly. I was trying to find a balance between being normal, staying true to myself, and making a memorable impression. I didn't want to be gimmicky, but I also didn't want to get lost in the shuffle of beautiful women. We had a brief but nice conversation before a producer schlepped Brad off and I headed back to the meet and greet.

When Chris Harrison walked into the room—it was the first time any of us had seen him thus far—there was an outbreak of girlie gasps. Everyone shut up quick. Wine glasses were put down. Dresses were smoothed out. Stray hairs were put in place. "You ladies look beautiful tonight," Chris began. "Thank you all for being here. We're about to get started for our first rose ceremony." *Finally*, I thought. It was three or four in the morning, and I was tired.

We were directed into another room where we were positioned on risers, being pulled by our elbows in all sorts of directions by a handful of producers.

"You here."

"You there."

"You switch with her."

We waited on those risers for a long time. I was pretty certain at some point I heard a rooster crow in the distance. Then Brad came out and gave a welcome or something-or-other kind of speech, and it was time for the rose roll call. Would I get one? I wasn't sure, but I hoped I would.

The process of waiting was awful. Brad would call out four or five names, drawing out each consonant and vowel annoyingly slow, and then walk out of the room for a few minutes, come back in, and call out another four or five names in the same unhurried manner. As I watched girl after girl walk down off a riser and accept their roses, the anticipation was eating away at me.

Finally, Brad said my name. "Emily, will you accept this rose?" I was one of the last girls called. As I accepted the long-stemmed beauty in my hand, the first thought that came to mind was, *Thank goodness I didn't get sent home the first day.* No offense to all *Bachelor* and *Bachelorette* contestants past, present, and future—including the ten girls who went home that night—but it seemed much less embarrassing to go home during the second rose ceremony.

I crawled into bed that night, mic pack finally off, dress still on, heels hanging off my feet, makeup smeared all over my face. Falling fast asleep as soon as my head hit the pillow, I didn't have any energy left to celebrate my victory. If the rest of the process was as exhausting as the first day, I needed as much stamina or as many gallons of Red Bull as I could find to get through the next round of one-on-ones, group dates, and who knew what else.

seven

When I woke up the next morning, besides regretting the makeup I never took off the night before—a terrible habit I'd grow accustomed to—I felt pretty good. Good, but nervous. Kind of like waking up the first day of summer camp. I smelled coffee somewhere and could hear the mingled racket of giggles and chatter and gossip on the floor below.

I sat up in bed, getting a good look at my room in the infamous Casa Bachelor. Everything always looks different in the morning light. Three plain bunk beds sandwiched into a tiny space that I shared with Michelle Money, Shawntel Newton, and Chantal O'Brien. Stuff was everywhere. Because the room was so small, it was like a black hole of jeans, tank tops, bikinis, makeup, moisturizer, flat irons, shoes, shoes, and more shoes. I couldn't take a step without my foot getting caught in a tank top or brassiere strap.

I think we were all able to sleep in that morning, which would prove a rare treat, before producers began milling around the house, grabbing girls left and right for some hoped-for juicy commentaries. Madison, the girl with the fangs, was still a hot topic. By midmorning, I definitely knew who she was. I finally said, "Fine, so do I think it's strange? Maybe, but who cares? Not everyone may get my look. So what?" I didn't see the point of making a spectacle out of Madison or any of the girls. We were all trying to feel our way around what was for most of us a place well outside of our comfort zones.

Obviously throughout the filming process, producers continued to ask us questions about Brad off camera and on, some of which were aired.

"How do you think last night went?"

"What did he smell like?"

"Did you have a connection?"

When it was my turn for an interview, I chose my words carefully. While I did like Brad and thought we had some chemistry, apparently so did a handful of other girls. I'd watched the show enough to see woman after woman, über-confident that whoever the Bachelor was at the time was totally in love with them and they were definitely going to get married and have babies and live happily ever after—and then, in the next shot, these same über-confident-in-love women were taking the walk of shame off the show, shoulders slumped, tears falling, feeling totally sucker-punched by love.

I had to approach this situation with wisdom, with caution. I needed time, space, to figure it all out. Even if my heart was going pitter-patter, I didn't want to blurt out my feelings to all of America without thinking about what I was saying. Even though I liked Brad, I needed to get to know him, which meant waiting for dates and one-on-one time. And that meant waiting around for Chris Harrison to show up and tell us what was next or waiting for a knock at the front door announcing the arrival of a date card to tell us which lucky woman, or women, would be spending time with Brad.

Group dates are the worst. They're so long, most starting at nine in the morning and ending well after midnight, and so boring, mainly because they are so long. Of course, I didn't know all this when I found out I was one of fifteen girls going on the first group date. I don't know what to call that, but fifteen girls and one Bachelor does not a date make.

The plan was to film scenes for a Red Cross public service announcement. Sounds fun, right? But for a non-actress like myself, it was a terrifying experience. I felt especially uncomfortable because I had such a heavy Southern accent and had to play a Spanish-speaking maid. Have you ever heard a Spanish-Southern accent? Yeah, it's pretty jarring. I also had to kiss Brad in one of the scenes, which felt out of place in real life. I tried to be a good sport about the whole thing, but between the lines I had trouble memorizing and trying very hard yet unsuccessfully to sound Spanish, my performance was a total flop. The director kept yelling at me and, not mincing words, finally said with much exasperation, "Emily, I would never, ever, have you at one of my auditions!" No kidding, Captain Obvious.

Then came the infamous make-out scene where Brad was on a bed and being mauled by Chantal and Britt. In true competitive form, these two bachelorettes took advantage of the opportunity and consequently sparked a whole lot of heat among the rest of the women on set. Michelle Money wasn't the only one ticked off. I was too. *This is not okay*, I thought. *I took time away from my girl for this baloney?* The PDA spectacle left a bad taste in my mouth about Brad and his character. And made me feel pretty gross.

Later, I got to spend time with Brad—and got a rose (yay!)—after former Bachelorette Ali Fedotowsky and her then-beau Roberto Martinez had interviewed all the ladies and fed him their opinions. I felt a stronger connection with Brad, seeing him in a different light outside of what had transpired on our group date. I admitted to him that I wasn't the type of woman to pour my soul out when I first meet someone. My mom used to always tell me, "Never chase, and never call a boy, Emily. Never."

I adopted that mentality in most of my relationships. Some would call it playing hard to get. But it wasn't a strategy or a ploy. It was part of my personality, and something that had been reinforced in me while growing up. Also, because I'd experienced loss in an extreme way, I remained guarded just enough that if a guy didn't return my affection, I wouldn't collapse under the weight of devastation. I felt the same way about the situation with Brad. If he wasn't chasing after me, I wasn't going to go out of my way to win his attention or affection.

When I got my first solo date card on the third episode, I was looking forward to spending more time with Brad and actually wanted to open up more, particularly about the important stuff—like Ricky's accident and the fact that I had a daughter.

Brad and I flew in a small plane to a beautiful vineyard. If I looked uncomfortable during the flight, it wasn't because I was having flashbacks of Ricky's accident. Though I'd always hated flying, I really wasn't particularly distraught on this trip. I'd been on little planes hundreds of times before.

When Brad and I got to talking about previous relationships during the beginning of our date, I seemed a big dud on TV, avoiding questions and trying, unskillfully, to switch gears. I wasn't scared to tell Brad about my daughter or her father's accident, but it wasn't an easy conversation to have.

When the moment came, my admission during dinner was far less climactic in reality than how the scene aired, with the dramatic music playing in the background and all. Brad was sweet about the whole thing. And I was very much relieved it was over. I felt disappointed when I watched the episode later; the date felt like another sob story, one of many sad tales that Brad was bombarded with on many of his dates. I felt sorry for the poor guy. I think we all owed him a nice dinner without him needing to hear about a tragic accident, an addicted family member, or any other heartbreaking story.

After that first one-on-one date, I thought Brad might not like me. Even though I was vulnerable and shared some of my personal story, it had taken so long for me to open up to him. I had this sinking feeling that Brad felt more comfortable around a woman who wasn't so reserved and was happy to divulge personal details and feelings. I didn't get to talk to him for about a week after our date, so the cocktail party before the fourth rose ceremony left me exasperated. I didn't know what Brad was thinking about me or our date.

And then, as I was sitting on the couch gabbing with the other girls during the soiree, his handsome self turned up round the corner, and he asked, picnic basket in hand, "Emily, do you have a second? Can I grab you really quickly?" Our moment was brief but sweet. Brad and I talked about Ricki (who, by the way, I was calling every day). Our time gave me the boost of confidence I needed to assure me Brad still considered me as a potential bachelorette. When I walked back into the house, I felt happy, giddy even. Not that I wanted to shout from the balcony how special Brad had made me feel. No need to stir unnecessary drama.

But my smile said it all. When I stepped into the living room where most of the girls had been before I was whisked away, you could hear a pin drop. The girls sat there, glaring. Nobody said a word. And then, one by one, they all left to go outside. I stood alone in the house, feeling paddled by a storm of insecurities, jealousies, and cattiness. This came with the reality-TV-show territory, I knew. But it sucked feeling so isolated by something you didn't do on purpose. Not knowing what to do next, I headed to the kitchen, a girl's best friend and worst enemy during emotional distress, where I threw back a glass of wine or two and some pizza.

We bachelorettes stayed in the Bachelor mansion for about two weeks. Outside of group dates, one-on-one dates, and solo interviews, there was a lot of waiting. We just sat around and got to know one another. The one incident I mentioned aside, I'd never been to college or had such a huge group of girlfriends, so staying in a house with many different kinds of women was actually super fun. When we weren't getting dolled up for dates, we were doing each other's nails and hair, talking, and eating. And yes, while the house bar was never lonely, I don't remember anyone getting drunk or downing shots during breakfast.

What I do remember is how quickly the house became a pigsty. Without much to do during the group dates that didn't include me, I cleaned—spraying, wiping, and bleaching to satisfy my OCD tendencies. Early on, I begged one of the producers for a vacuum. Can you imagine how much hair a house full of twenty or so women and their extensions will generate?

I'm grossed out just thinking about it. During one of the rose ceremonies, I couldn't even pay attention to who Brad was calling because I was zoned in on a hot dog, no bun, on the floor wrapped in a tangled heap of long hair. One time when I was cleaning the bathroom, I was greeted by a half-eaten bowl of cereal in the shower stall. Now come on! Who is really that busy they need to eat in the shower?

Aside from some really awful housekeeping habits, I loved the camaraderie in the house. Ashley S. made me laugh like no other. Ashley H. was sweet and incredibly smart. Though I had mixed feelings about getting to know a funeral home director, I fast discovered Shawntel's heart of gold and encouraging spirit. Keltie was a girl's girl, down-to-earth, funny, and real. She was a health nut, homeopathic this and organic that, and always carried around this medieval-looking Pilates contraption.

I became close to Michelle Money and Lisa Morrisey. Lisa was quiet, like me, but very cool, and we had an almost immediate bond. We'd always hide whenever we were called down for rose ceremonies, sneaking our pajama bottoms on under our dresses. Michelle was a lot sweeter than how she came across on the show. She always helped the girls out with their hair and makeup, many times even before hers was done. When I found out she was a mom, I leaned on her for support. I was grateful to have a friend who could understand how much I missed my little girl.

There wasn't much cat fighting in the house. In fact, most of us got along so well, I was convinced this season would be the most boring of them all. I did have one confrontation with Ashley H. that didn't air. She had a bit too much to drink during one particular group date and acted out of character. She later apologized to Brad, bringing up the excuse that she was upset about an ex-boyfriend who had recently passed away. When I had heard this, something in me was triggered. I felt she used the victim card, and that made me angry.

Of course, my feelings had nothing to do with her. Looking back, I got so angry because of my own insecurities and what I'd been through when Ricky died. A bunch of us girls were talking about the situation, and in the middle of our groaning, Ashley H. walked in. Every one of us clammed up immediately, an obvious sign we were talking about her. Ashley wasn't dumb. She knew what time it was.

When she asked us what was going on, I told her how I felt. That I didn't like her using a situation as an excuse and yada, yada, yada. I went on and on, not taking a breath. I was all claws at that point, not showing Ashley any grace or empathy, and the rest of the girls in the room, who were watching this scene unfold before them, couldn't believe that I, the least confrontational girl in the house, had turned into a raging bull. I wish I had kept my mouth shut.

As quiet as the room was before Ashley walked in to face the firing squad of belittling talk, if it was possible, it got even quieter. Ashley didn't say much. She just stood there, tears falling. After saying my piece, I walked away and hid in my room, feeling very alone, wondering if everyone hated me.

I had hurt Ashley's feelings, and I was sorry for that. I had no right to call her out in a room full of people. It was disrespectful. And no matter what I was going through internally at the time or what I had been through in the past, I should have looked inward instead of blowing up outwardly at someone else.

An hour or so later, I felt terrible and asked the producers if I could talk to Ashley off camera. My wish was granted. "I'm very sorry," I told her. "I know what you've been through, and I'm sorry you had to go through it. I'm sorry I judged you. I know better than that."

Ashley responded in kind and sweetly accepted my apology. We talked for a while that night, her asking me questions about Ricky and the accident, both of us sharing the devastating effects of grief. Surprisingly, the whole situation, as ugly and hard as it was, brought us closer. She became a friend and we stayed in touch after that show. Two years later, I was thrilled she found true love with J. P. on season 7 of *The Bachelorette* and was honored to attend their wedding.

Something similar happened with Chantal, the confrontation part, at least. She came home from a one-on-one date with Brad, and while typically the remaining girls in the house would pepper whoever came back from dates with questions and ask for juicy details, this one time no one said a word to Chantal. I think we could all tell Brad had some deep feelings for her and we were understandably jealous. I could tell Chantal was upset and later told her, off camera as well, that I was sorry, that I didn't want her to think everyone was talking about her, and that we were all jealous and tired and allowing our emotions to get the best of us. All she said was, "Thanks." Our exchange did not include a kumbaya moment.

Being on *The Bachelor* is not your everyday, garden-variety experience. Cameramen are everywhere, and producers looking for entertaining and air-worthy sound bites are wandering around asking you questions about how you feel about your experience, Brad, and the other girls. And even though after a while you start to forget that you're being constantly watched and filmed, sooner or later your emotions start to run wild.

It doesn't take long to get caught up in the drama, the suspicions that the other girls in the house are out to get you, or your man, which of course is partially true. And because being part of the show means giving up access to a phone, a computer, the Internet—basically contact with the outside world—you don't have the support of others outside of your housemates to find strength, a sounding board, or simply a sanity check. Even if you are not a competitive person, like me, this instinctual aggressive nature erupts, at least internally, and you start to get a bit miffed that other women are competing for the man of your dreams. I know, you think you'd understand this obvious fact going in, right? But in the beginning, you're so blinded by what could be a potential fairy tale that reality doesn't quite sink in. When it does, you just want to be the one who's picked. You want to be the last girl standing. Yeah, that happened to me. I can't say exactly when, but it did.

When it was time to leave the mansion and head to Las Vegas for a six-week journey around the world, I was itching for a change of scenery, for a breather from the fast-and-furious emotions of being in the house. And, of course, I was happy to clutch yet another rose that gave me the continued chance to get to know Brad. The rules of the game remained unchanged. We were contractually bound to keep our mouths shut as unauthorized spoilers could damage the show. Unfortunately, somehow information would get discovered and leaked. Can't control everything, I guess. So with the ground rules reinforced and bags packed, fourteen of us said good-bye to Los Angeles and hello to Sin City.

I had been to Las Vegas once before and was familiar with the lights, the glamour, and the nonstop party climate, but I'd never before noticed the mountains. Our Sky Villa in the Aria Resort bragged some pretty impressive mountainous scenery, transporting me far away from this crazy road trip for love. Ever since Ricky's accident, I've had a love-hate relationship with mountains. While a part of me despises them, their looming peaks reminding me of his tragic death, I'm likewise fascinated by them. Maybe it's because I grew up in the great outdoors of West Virginia and seeing them brings me back to the simplicity of childhood. A carefree life, wind on my face, breathing in fresh air.

That first morning in Vegas I woke up to the view of the mountains in a bedroom I shared with Michelle M. and Lisa. Immediately overcome with peace, I noticed the irony. Because the floor-to-ceiling windows overlooked the distant peaks, and not the Strip and the lights and the bevy of fun and frolic below, my mind was drawn to the Creator. I thought of how awesome God is, how He forms and appreciates beauty. How even in a city famous for its unscrupulous reputation, His majesty could still be known. I prayed a lot in Vegas, many times in that huge bathroom tub, staring out into the mountains while scrubbing off the last bits of spray tan from my body.

The second day in Vegas offered a group date, probably one of the worst during the whole show, but not for the reason you might expect. Jackie, Lisa, Marissa, Alli, Chantal, Britt, Michelle, and I drove out of the city in the limo, as usual, without a clue where we were headed. The minute I saw the huge Las Vegas Motor Speedway sign I cringed. This was where Ricky had been involved in the 2002 accident that ended his career as a race-car driver. I felt upset, but not at the fact that I would spend the date at this racetrack.

Noticing my plaster smile, Brad pulled me aside to talk.

"I'm worried about you," he said as we both sat down on the Astroturf in the middle of the track.

"I'm fine," I said.

Brad wasn't convinced. "Are you?"

"I mean, I'm so excited just to be here with you."

"I saw your face change," Brad prodded further.

"I don't want you to think I'm not grateful to be here, but honestly, I just wanted to move on from the whole NASCAR world because it's so much a part of my life in Charlotte."

"What got you into NASCAR?" Brad asked. "Was it your fiancé?"

And then the revelation. "Ricky was a race-car driver and then moved into an owner position. The Vegas racetrack is what ended his career as a driver." I fought a few tears but continued. "It just felt like, you think you leave it behind and then I come here . . ." My voice trailed off as Brad nodded.

"Yeah, I understand," he said. "I kinda feel like a jerk."

"No," I assured him. "This is why I did not want to have this conversation." And boy, how I wanted our talk to end. I wanted Brad to know there was more to me than being a mom who experienced a tragic event. I didn't want to make the NASCAR date into something it wasn't, a big deal because of Ricky. So while I'd never before been in the driver's seat of a race car, I did my laps. I wanted it to be over as fast as possible.

Lisa, along with Marissa, got sent home at the rose cere-mony in Vegas. Michelle and I were sad to see Lisa go. Knowing how close the three of us were, and even though this wasn't the norm, they allowed the three of us to spend a few minutes saying good-bye.

That night, still feeling upset over Lisa's departure, bummed about losing a friend, I thought about Brad. I really liked him as a person. I'd only been on a few dates with him, so I couldn't say I was head over heels, but I was optimistic that maybe, just maybe, he was the one. Looking back, I won-der if I just wanted so bad to find love through this experience, rather than focusing on determining whether or not Brad was the right fit for my future.

In Vegas, the girls started noticing the special treatment he seemed to be giving me. At first, I pooh-poohed away their comments, but then I started noticing it myself. He did go out of his way to get to know me or just ask how I was doing. I started feeling pretty good about him, about us, at that point, finally admitting that maybe I was experiencing a flutter or two of butterflies in my stomach. But I was definitely not going to publicize the kindling of my feelings. My gut still screamed, *Proceed slowly! Use caution!*

Things were about to heat up on our road trip around the world, starting first with beautiful Costa Rica.

"Isn't this the perfect place to fall in love?"

"Love is a lot like traveling. You never know where it's going to take you."

"I can't wait to get a stamp of love in my passport!"

Any of these sound familiar? Excuse me while I retch. Our passageway out of the States included any number, or variety, of the above clichés. At first, I thought it was annoying, but after a while, it became funny. I mean really, who says these things in real life? They're hilariously corny! As ridiculous as some of the questions producers asked us seemed, they were talented men and women who were just doing their jobs, making a great show. While, sure, some scenes were more guided than natural, the producers weren't a bunch of hungry wolves out only to suck whatever scandalous or sensational thoughts or actions they could from us bachelorettes. I know for a fact that some of the producers truly believed the show could match two people for a lasting love.

Our time in Costa Rica was a hot, rainy mess. Ali, Michelle, Ashley H., Jackie, Shawntel, Britt, and I stayed at the Springs Resort & Spa, a breathtaking hotel nestled in a mountain ridge and only four miles away from and with a magnificent view of the Arenal Volcano. Our villa was right in the middle of the jungle, edged by bold tropical flowers and lush trees. And though the open windows welcomed the scent of paradise, without air-conditioning it was our only source of relief from the sweltering temperatures. It was hot, people. I don't remember ever sweating so much in my life. And this is coming from a girl who's lived in Florida!

The heat and jungle atmosphere were also very inviting to a number of large spiders with long, spindly legs as well as giant buzzing bugs that scurried around on the walls, over our luggage, and yes, sometimes even into our hair. By the end of the first day, I realized I had to be on my A-game at all times, wary of creepy crawlies that would appear out of nowhere, no doubt getting their kicks from our ear-splitting screams.

The glamour of being on *The Bachelor* was wearing off of most of us by this time. Jet-setting to exotic locations aside, being in this kind of situation gets a little hairy the more you, little by little, invest into the man of the hour. For me, my emotions were beginning to lose some balance. I started getting pelted by anxiety and bushwhacked by jealousy (more on that in a minute).

Remember how I said I love the mountains? This was still true in Costa Rica, to a certain extent. It was pouring rain on our first group date, which demanded us to rappel down the side of a mountain on a flimsy rope. Looking up at a mountain is an entirely different thing than going down one. Maybe this sounds boring, but no, I'm not an adventurer. I'm not the girl who says with a beaming smile that she is "up for anything!" I don't rock climb. I don't ski. And the only water sport I'll participate in is floating on a tube in wave- and wake-free water. Rappelling down massive waterfalls? Not so much fun. Especially not on a date. And not on one where you're already covered head to toe in a drenching plastic-bag poncho feigning excitement while raindrops pound into your eyeballs.

When it was my turn, the minute I bounced off the side of the mountain, I got even more drenched by the violent spray of the waterfalls. It was like rappelling while someone blasts you with a gushing garden hose at point-blank range. At one point, between the driving rain and the falls, so much water was pouring down my face I could barely see and forgot to kick off the mountain wall as the rope lowered me further down. I hung there in limbo, soaked to my underthings, screaming for someone to "get me out of here" until one of the locals was able to rescue my wet self. I was proud that I didn't chicken out, but felt pretty embarrassed because I looked like a troll. I tried to avoid Brad the rest of the outing and couldn't wait to get back to the dry hotel, exotic creepy crawlers and all.

Later that night, all of us hit the pool. It was my first time being filmed while in a bikini, and I may not have looked it, but I was very uncomfortable. Ever since being pregnant, I've been insecure about my body (tropical drinks help numb the insecurity). We were having fun, drinking, and being silly when Brad came up and asked me to swim with him to the other side of the pool. You don't see this on TV, but the first part of our conversation stumbled around very awkwardly. As we dipped our legs in the warm water, I said, "I'm starting to really like you, Brad, and that's super crazy." Good, right? I'm opening up, being more vulnerable. And then I said, "But I do things in relationships, you know, to sabotage them."

I know—what on earth, right? The funny thing was, it wasn't really true. Right before I had gotten into the pool that evening, some of the producers asked why my other relation-ships had failed. I didn't give an answer, but my brain started spinning its wheels. Sure, after Ricky's accident I had dated a few guys here and there, but I never fell in love, and none of the relationships—if you could even call them that—lasted more than a few weeks. So while Brad and I stared into the gleaming pool, the other bikini-clad gorgeous women eyeing us with curiosity, I think my insecurity got the best of me. And I babbled, definitely putting foot into mouth. I felt so weirded out after the "confession," I cut bait. I jumped into the pool, hoping Brad and the cameras would focus elsewhere.

No such luck. The minute I surfaced, cameras were still on me. Which stunk for two reasons: one, I felt pretty silly after the conversation with Brad, and two, the jump in the pool did a number on my eye makeup, the mascara lumping around my eyes in a thick layer of mess. I knew I looked like a raccoon, so I tried to keep my back to the camera while they filmed me and Brad talking more—me trying to spit out how I didn't want to ruin my chance with him and him eventually kissing me.

Before the night ended, Brad announced he wasn't giving out any roses. The girls scratched their heads at that one. While I didn't expect one, given our unpleasant talk, I had the sinking feeling, once again, that I had scared him off, yes, even in light of our smooch fest. Feeling emotionally drained, I went to bed.

The next day, Michelle told me she had snuck out to visit Brad in his villa the night before. Chantal had come home wearing Brad's shirt from a one-on-one date, and Michelle took it upon herself to return it for Chantal, thus surprising him in his room. I laughed when she told me, thinking what a bold move it was. But I also got jealous. Michelle was aggressive and openly showered Brad with attention, making crystal clear she really, really liked him. The way she was so vulnerable with him made my guarded self feel insecure. Brad didn't seem to mind her approach. It was obvious he dug her. And that made me worried. But it also made me think that because Michelle and I were so different, if Brad had the hots for her, then he was probably not the guy for me. And if that was the case, well, I had no choice but to move on.

The conversation Brad and I had had at the pool weighed heavily on me. I felt as though I needed to redeem myself, to assure Brad I liked him and wasn't going to allow a little fear or reservation to make me hightail it to Timbuktu.

I was filled with anxiety during the cocktail party before the rose ceremony. So when Brad and I had the chance to talk alone, I was ecstatic. This was my opportunity, my time to set the record straight.

Brad and I sat on a hammock, swinging slowly side to side as a light tropical breeze settled around us. I looked into his handsome face and in that moment could sense the pressure he was under. I felt bad for him because all these girls were looking to him—some demanding, others more heartfelt—for answers. I know he signed on to do the show and had some anticipation that when a handful of girls really like you and you have to ultimately choose one, things are bound to get messy and complicated. Still, this was a lot of drama, emotionally and otherwise, to sift through.

It wasn't easy for me to gush, but I did my best. "Brad," I began. "I know you can't give me reassurance about our relationship, but I can tell you that I do have feelings for you. I know I'm a bit more shy and don't put myself out there like the other girls, but I do like you. A lot." I'll never forget, as my legs stretched across his lap and Brad held my hand, he started rubbing the ring finger on my left hand.

Then he said, "I've really tried my best to show you how I feel about you," while continuing to gently caress my ring finger. It was the most amazing, intimate moment I'd had with Brad yet. And this time, it scared me to death.

So, sure, I was finally able to redeem that awful conversation and, yes, I got a rose that night. I should have felt confident, right? Optimistic? If not floating high on a cloud of euphoria? But as I started journaling before I went to bed, doubt whispered in my ear.

Maybe this is all in my head.

Maybe Brad's lying.

Maybe he said the same thing to Michelle or Chantal or some other girl.

Maybe I'm overanalyzing everything.

One of my favorite producers on the show nicknamed me Doomsday Maynard. He figured out pretty quickly that I'm my own worst enemy. I have a very annoying tendency to doubt, to worry, to fear, to question, to not get hyped up when something good happens for fear the second I blink, it's going to get snatched away, and I'll be left standing, the butt of some sick and twisted divine joke. In this case, there was nothing I could do other than try my best to be open to the possibility of love and wait. Wait for our next destination. And wait for another rose to settle my anxiety that this wasn't just a made-for-TV relationship.

eight

By the time the six of us (Ashley, Michelle, Chantal, Shawntel, Britt, and I) reached the turquoise shores of Anguilla, I could have stuck my head in and kissed the sprawling, sandy Caribbean beach—if it wasn't weird . . . or gross. I don't think I'd seen the sun during the entire week we spent in Costa Rica. It was pretty depressing! But hey, I didn't sign up for a vacation, now, did I? What can you say about Anguilla? It's gorgeous. A tropical paradise. Sun and surf and refreshing breezes and stunning shades of blue everywhere you look.

While we were traveling to all these cool places, there were some repercussions from constantly being on the move, adapting to different time zones, different foods, different environments—all while being sequestered from the world and clustered with the same group of girls, never knowing when you're going to be sent home. So far, outside of getting to know Brad better and hanging with the other girls around pools and hot tubs and giving each other manicures and sharing beauty tips, there wasn't much to do but eat and drink. Eat and drink while we were giving pedis. Eat and drink while we were curling hair. Eat and drink while we were talking about

Brad. Then, eat more and drink more. Sleep wasn't high on the priority list, and while I would usually crash earlier than most of the girls, there were plenty of times I'd get by on only a few hours of sleep.

I was so sleep deprived at one point, I remembered the sleeping pill I had packed, just in case. I was desperate for at least one night to go to bed at a decent hour and not wake up like the living dead. After taking the pill, I finally fell asleep around 3:00 a.m. Only four hours later, barely enough time for the effects of the medication to subside, I was abruptly woken up by a producer shouting to my sleeping beauty self, "Chris Harrison is downstairs. Let's go!"

I don't remember getting out of bed. I don't remember putting on shoes. I don't remember climbing down the stairs. But I made it, sitting on the couch with the rest of my fresh-eyed and perky companions, most of whom looked like they'd been up for hours. I remember looking down at one point, right before I nodded off in my medicated stupor, and noticing I had forgotten to put on pants. I was wearing a long flannel nightshirt, undies, and UGGs. That's it. My observation was brief, however, as I immediately settled into a five-second snooze fest before I heard Chris say, "Emily? Emily?"

I immediately gained enough consciousness to open my droopy eyes wide and smile. "Oh yes, I'm sorry. Um, what's that?" I mumbled, a little too cheerily. Chris continued to say something I don't remember as I nodded off again, trying very unsuccessfully to stay alert.

Next thing I heard was Chris asking one of the producers, "Is Emily okay?"

"Yup, yup. Here I am!" I piped up again, absolutely clueless to what was going on around me. By the time the sleeping pill wore off, I was petrified they would show the clip and I'd be portrayed as a pill-popping drunk or something. Luckily, in the episode that aired, I was faded in the background.

I had a one-on-one date with Brad in Anguilla. We whirred above the island in a helicopter, landing on a remote section of beach where we picnicked, swam, and cuddled. I felt comfortable with Brad, a little less guarded.

"I like it out here," Brad said, admiring the idyllic scene around us.

"Me too."

He was quiet for a few seconds. "What are you thinking?" I asked.

"Uh, this is a really cool view."

"It is really pretty."

"Can I tell you something? I get nervous around you."

"I do too!"

"I kick myself either for fumbling my words or to be honest not kissing you," he opened up as we sipped on champagne and munched on fancy cheese.

"This is scary," I admitted.

"What scares you?" he asked.

"Getting my heart broken, but I know to fall in love I have to let down my guard."

"Em, I care for you so much and I take things slowly because I like you. This is me. I move slowly. I care more for you than I should probably even say right now." And grabbing my face in his hands, Brad kissed me.

At dinner, lulled by the calming sound of the tide as it rolled up and gracefully sprawled over the shore, Brad told me he wanted to meet Ricki. I let out an apparently loud sigh, not feeling it at all. I know my hesitation disappointed him, but Ricki was my life. She hadn't met any guy I dated, and really, I had only known him for a few short weeks. So for as many deep feelings as I had to want to get to know him more, and as hopeful as I was that maybe, just maybe, we could both fall in love and live happily ever after, I wasn't ready for him to meet Ricki. She was the portal to my life, my world. She was mine.

Brad was sweet and understanding. Apart from his handsome features and bulging biceps, these two characteristics drew me closer to him. I was elated when he told me I was getting a hometown date, which was scheduled for the next week. The announcement came as a shock to the producers. Not that he picked me, but that he actually told me so before the rose ceremony. All Bachelors and Bachelorettes were sternly warned not to spoil any surprises on camera. Brad got in trouble for this one, but it upped my confidence that his feelings for me were real.

We sailed through the rest of the evening in a romantic blur. If you're wondering whether or not it's awkward to kiss while cameramen are filming, uh, definitely. But sometimes they are far enough away that you forget they're there. I enjoyed cuddling with Brad as moonlight glazed the ocean's surface, but the captivating scene wasn't strong enough for me to ignore the obvious. As Brad and I canoodled, five other women sat in a beautiful house waiting, hoping, to do the same.

October 24 rolled around while I was still in Anguilla. It marked the sixth anniversary of Ricky's death. I had mentioned this to the producers, but not to the other girls. I didn't want to make a big deal out of it or draw any more attention to my story. When the anniversaries had approached in the past, I'd always just checked out, spent a good part of the week aimlessly plodding around in a dark funk. This year was different. I felt washed by an unusual, a good, sense of peace. It was the first time I was doing something in my life to move forward after losing the love of my life. It felt hopeful.

Before we left the beautiful island, it was rose ceremony time. Brad opted to nix the cocktail party because his mind was made up on whom he was going to send home, after saying good-bye to Britt earlier that afternoon. I was sad when Michelle was sent home, though I knew what a strong woman she was and was confident she'd be fine. I was going to miss my buddy, for sure, but I also knew that for the next few weeks, the remaining bachelorettes would be separated and not allowed to interact. I wouldn't have gotten to hang out with my friend anyway.

Michelle's exit interview was hilarious. She was as smart as she was sassy and sexy. She and I stayed in touch after the filming ended.

And then there were four.

It's a great honor to be given a hometown date. And it's also exciting. A chance to hop off the crazy train of emotional upheaval and constant traveling to be surrounded by those you love (though you are not allowed to talk to your family about anything having to do with the show). Watching previous episodes, I'd seen how fun these dates were, being with family who are in your corner. But when arrangements were being made for Chantal to fly out to Seattle, Ashley to Maine, and Shawntel to California, and the girls were squealing with delight at being able to break at home, I was less enthusiastic.

Seeing Ricki, of course, was the highlight. I couldn't wait to scoop her up in my arms. But for various reasons, none of my family members, nor the Hendricks, were willing to share the experience with me. This made me sad. I had visions of Chantal, Ashley, and Shawntel showing Brad off to their perfect families in their perfect houses chowing down their perfect lunches and dinners and touring their perfect towns. In comparison, my hometown date seemed, well, lonely, a sentiment that only reinforced my sad and depressing story line. And I wasn't 100 percent sold on Brad meeting my daughter. It felt fake, like playing house.

I missed Ricki something fierce. And I was feeling so conflicted at how far along I'd come on the show and that my relationship—or however it could be defined—with Brad was progressing. I liked him, but loved my daughter more. And my homesickness trumped what could possibly be love. Some of my family members were even trying hard to persuade me to call the whole thing off and come home. The producers knew all this and were generous to film my hometown date first and then fly Ricki and me to New York City where we would spend a few days together waiting for the other girls to arrive to film the rose ceremony prior to being whisked off to another unknown destination.

I can't even begin to tell you what it felt like to have Ricki in my arms back in Charlotte. Her bright smile, her dreamy eyes, her shampoo-scented hair, her giddy chatter, her little hands clutching mine—I soaked it all in. Home. That's what it felt like. Home. Seeing my mom and being able to catch up with her was another blessing. Though I couldn't share any of my experience, none of the nitty-gritty details, I was happy to see my mom (not saying one way or the other that I did or didn't abide by the contract by keeping mum during my time with her).

We had a heart-to-heart during some anxiously awaited alone time, and she admitted one of the reasons she opted off the show was because she wouldn't be able to handle what could end up as a heartbreaking situation for me, having to go through two months of intensity only to be broken up with in front of millions of Americans on national TV. It would have torn her up. As a mom, I understood, and still appreciated the fact that she supported me, though in this case off camera.

Ricki meeting Brad, who I presented to her as merely a friend, was more uncomfortable, awkward, and weird than how it looked on the actual episode, which was a good deal of uncomfortable, awkward, and weird. With cameramen and producers scattered around my house, the whole shebang felt so orchestrated. Again, like playing house. Reality as a single mom is not just about flying kites in a park and sweetly tucking in an adorable little girl. As I told Brad later that night, parenthood involves a lot of not-so-sweet things, like taking care of them in the middle of the night when they're sick. And dealing with annoying tantrums. And needing to travel to mostly kid-friendly places. And not being able to be totally spontaneous. And not being able to party and kick back for the night because you can sleep in the next morning.

Obviously, I knew all this because I was in the trenches. I didn't want to scare the poor guy off. I liked him. I did. But my feelings were spotted with the realities of raising a child, the realities of life's inevitable messes, the reality behind the cameras. I wondered if Brad was ready to accept, to even welcome, the sacrifices that came along with being a stepparent. I hoped he was, but I wasn't confident. Perhaps I came off a bit too strong, but when it comes to my little girl, I'll always err on the side of being overly cautious.

After spending a day or two in Charlotte, Ricki and I took off for New York City, while Chantal, Ashley, and Shawntel prepared for their hometown dates. I needed that break with my girl and time off from filming to feel normal again.

Ricki was the focus of the entire week. We did whatever she wanted to do, which included a trip on Broadway to see *The Lion King*, a day at the American Girl Place (really, you need at least a day to browse through every inch of the three-floored, forty-two-thousand-square-foot doll heaven), and a visit to the fabulous Serendipity where we stuffed ourselves with hot fudge sundaes and slurped frozen hot chocolate. It was a magical time.

The rose ceremony was planned for the night that Ricki was scheduled to fly back home. My mother flew up from Charlotte so she could travel back to North Carolina with my baby. I needed, and appreciated, those few days of relative ordinariness, just being a mom, trekking through the Big Apple like a giddy tourist. I rode with Mom and Ricki to the airport, the three of us drenched in a deluge of tears and I love yous.

That night in New York City, sans my little girl, was the rose ceremony where Brad said good-bye to Shawntel, who was shocked to be sent home. After Brad took some time to talk to her and I guess explain his choice, which really doesn't help any girl who feels sucker punched by rejection, he told us we were going to—wait for it, wait for it—South Africa!

Wowzers! As we three girls shrieked for joy in the Manhattan penthouse suite, I remembered the abysmal stack of questionnaires I had to fill out when I was first being screened for the show. One of the matchmaking-type questions posed was to describe my ideal, most fun date. I didn't have to think long and hard for that one. *Ride an elephant in Africa*, I scribbled. I hoped that was on the list! Chantal, Ashley, and I said quick good-byes, paired up with now individual producers, and prepared for our separate twenty-hour-plus journeys to South Africa. The next time we'd see one another would be the forthcoming rose ceremony. Talk about weird.

I was buddied up with a producer, a Middle-Eastern–looking guy with crazy hair who wore ponchos and bandanas. Incredibly sweet and funny, he quickly became my best friend throughout the rest of filming. After about a full day of traveling from the States, enduring long layovers and long flights, passing through multiple time zones, and finally touching down in South Africa, my producer and I left the airport, hopping in an open, rugged Jeep driven by a local. We headed toward our hotel, Casa do Sol, located in the province of Mpumalanga and about fifteen minutes from Kruger National Park, one of the largest game reserves in Africa.

Because our hotel was located within a nature and game reserve and next door to an elephant sanctuary, we were given ample opportunities to gawk at majestic elephants and giraffes while they roamed their natural habitat. As we rolled into the driveway of our hotel, a massive and wrinkled elephant crossed straight across our path, playfully swinging its giant trunk in a graceful cadence. My eyes widened as I shrieked like a little kid. "Can we ride one?" I begged, grabbing my producer's arm so hard, my fingernails on the verge of leaving marks.

He smiled knowingly, but shook his head. "Not today, you can't."

Our resort reminded me of being in Cancun, hence the Mexican name I suppose. Though we were in the wild, the accommodations were luxurious. Lush gardens, tranquil pools, charming cobbled paths, and terracotta Spanish-tiled roofs colored the villas. It was breathtaking. When the sun set that evening, I grabbed my journal and sat on my bedroom balcony staring into the midnight sky. I was too mesmerized by the scene above to start thinking about Brad being on his date with Chantal or Ashley. Sprawled over a sea of black stretched a thick, sparkling blanket of stars, millions and millions of them, some forming staggering clusters that released a powerful shine. I'd never before seen anything like that—and going back to South Africa to see those wonders of the night sky again is high on my bucket list.

I was grateful for the opportunity to be in South Africa, to get a glimpse of raw nature, untouched, unfiltered, and so mind-blowing. Being alone on the balcony, gazing into heaven, I loved what felt like an escape. I don't want to come off as being unappreciative, but by this point, I was so tired. I was tired of sharing Brad with other women (and yes, I know that was the point of the show). I was tired of overanalyzing every conversation I had with him. And I was tired of being alone. I wanted to either be with Brad or go home. I just wanted normal life back.

The next morning, the South African sun greeted me with

muted shades of orange, pink, and red, along with a troupe of playful monkeys clowning around on my balcony. Doing my first interview of the day proved difficult, with the curious animals screeching and whooping as they swung from one side of the roof to the other, swatting the boom mic in the process. It was cute to watch, but the amusing diversion became annoying when we had to do a dozen-plus takes.

By the time Brad and I had our date, I was so ready for my turn at alone time with him. As I waited in what seemed the middle of nowhere for Brad to whisk me away, imagine my surprise when I heard the trumpeting roar of an elephant in the midst of snapping branches. Yup, I almost peed my pants. And there was Brad, doing what I've always dreamed of doing—riding an elephant! I was shaking, a crazy mixture of nerves and excitement, as a few locals hoisted me up onto this ten-thousand-pound animal, its ears slapping wildly against tough, wrinkly skin. I was glad to share this moment with Brad. We laughed like giddy schoolgirls as we rocked side to side in time with the elephant's surprisingly graceful gait.

After the ride of a lifetime, Brad and I were led to a dock that overlooked a large, muddy pond. The brown body of water was cluttered by elephants of varying sizes that rolled around, played with one another, and trumpeted squeals. One of the producers asked us to go for a swim, but I refused. Only a few seconds earlier, I had seen an elephant relieve itself of a giant pile of you-know-what and, excuse me, um, what now? You want me to go swimming in that? I think not.

My feelings for Brad were the same. I liked him. He was warm, kind, sweet, a gentleman. I admired the same qualities now as I had when we first started getting to know each other. Yet, he wasn't as funny as I wanted him to be, and even though we had a great time together, he always seemed a bit uptight. Whenever I would mention this to the producers, they reassured me with things like, "Oh, Emily, he's just so nervous around you." I thought it was sweet. *Ahhh, he really likes me!* But really, it was a classic sign that I needed to get to know him, us, a whole lot better.

My emotions were tangled in a debris-ridden rubble of confusion. It was hard to distinguish what was real and what was reality TV. When you're filming a show like *The Bachelor*, the two get intertwined pretty quickly into an indistinguishable mess. While I felt strongly that I had made the right decision to be cast on the show, things were moving way too fast for me to process my emotions in a healthy and wise way. Reflecting back, I think I just wanted to want to fall in love with Brad. I think I wanted to want to be engaged to him. Because, really, I had no business talking about a serious relationship, let alone marriage, to someone I had just met. But the pressure for me to explain my feelings to Brad, the ones I wasn't sure I had, mounted each day and made me think twice about what I was getting myself into.

I was tired of what was starting to feel like work. I tried hard to make Brad comfortable by opening up and being more vocal about my feelings, but the fact was, I was one of three girls now, and I didn't want to spend the last few days chasing him around like a little puppy. I sure wouldn't act like that with a guy in real life.

While I didn't plan on spending the night with Brad, I couldn't wait to spend time with him off camera in the infamous suite. Before I stepped into the room after dinner, my producer pulled me aside and said, "Emily, we need you to be more open with him. Show him how you feel."

Brad and I sat on the wicker couch in the Fantasy Suite, surrounded by producers and cameramen, talking to each other but basically waiting for everyone to leave. It had been a long day and we wanted to relax, alone. Being in the suite was a light at the end of the tunnel. But nobody would leave. The crew stayed, filming. Watching. Waiting.

And that's when I did it. "Brad," I said, "I am falling in love with you." Actually, I said, "I'm absolutely, completely falling in love with you."

We talked for a while. Brad and I both opened up about our past relationships, enjoying each other's company. It was sweet.

The next rose ceremony took place on a dock overlooking a river occupied by hordes of hippos watching us suspiciously as they swam stealthily around the peaceful waters. Chantal and I waited for Ashley to make her appearance so the three of us could wait together for Brad to hand out the remaining two roses. I could tell something was wrong with Ashley when she came toward us. She looked as though she'd been crying all night. The sun beat down strong on my shoulders as Brad made his way down the dock and, not saying a word to us, reached out for Ashley's hands. Together they walked away. I didn't know what they were doing or where they were going.

As Brad and Ashley left, the cameras zoned in on Chantal and me, who had to stand and wait, and wait, and wait, until the pair came back. We couldn't talk to each other, so we stood in silence, the background of the wild, chirping, snorting, and howling engulfing the quiet. Ashley never came back, just Brad.

After he announced that Chantal and I were the final two

lucky women left standing, he asked the producers if he and I could spend some time together, alone, off camera. Graciously, they agreed. (Side note: That was the last I saw of Chantal.)

I don't know if it was the romantic evening we had shared the night before, the emotional high of being the "chosen one," or what, but I was getting more excited about this whole thing coming to what seemed to be a very hopeful close. It's amazing how powerful emotions are, how quickly they can change or be influenced.

Capetown was next, our final destination. There I met Brad's family, his mom and two brothers and their wives, who were really nice and made for wonderful company. On one of our outings, his brother said something like, "So have you poked the bear yet?" I didn't know what he meant or what he was talking about, so I just laughed it off and started talking about something else. I realized what Brad's brother was saying toward the end of my last date with Brad, the one before the final rose ceremony.

Before that Last Chance Date, producers had been pushing me to dig a little deeper with Brad. "Ask him harder questions," one said.

"Like what?" I asked. For Pete's sake, I felt like Brad and I had talked about everything already.

Reeling from so many different emotions, I was filled with doubt by the time Brad and I reunited for the Last Chance Date. When he and I had a chance to sit down and talk after soaking in the Capetown scenery via helicopter, I started, unintentionally, poking the bear.

The conversation focused on the topic of Ricki. "I can't wait to be a stepdad," Brad said, grinning.

I nodded and began my passionate interrogation. "Well, what exactly does that mean?"

For the next few minutes, Brad would offer how ready he was to be a father. And I would question his statements, posing more questions of my own, and reiterating that parenting wasn't a walk in the park. The same conversation kept cycling. And cycling. And cycling.

The minute I emotionally stepped away from the moment and could begin to see what was a pointless conversation, I noticed Brad getting angry. He kept touching the sides of his face, shifting his eyes down, giving me a little less eye contact. I'd never before seen him do that. Once he started turning red, it was obvious he was on the verge of losing control but was trying hard to contain his emotions. Yup, I had poked the bear.

When Brad left the room the first time, the time you don't see on the episode, I sat on the couch wondering what on earth I had done. I was confused. On one hand, I was totally turned off by his reaction. On the other hand, the more I thought about the situation, the more I could understand he was probably at his breaking point. Being on the show is demanding. And Brad was under a lot of pressure. Eventually, he did come back and gave me a stiff hug to end our evening.

I went to bed that night questioning our relationship, as well as my confidence in Brad picking me now that I had just really ticked him off. I had woken up early the next morning, spending time alone on my balcony, when I saw Brad on his balcony a floor down from me and over to the left. "Hey," I called out. Brad turned his head and replied a stale, "Hey," before hurriedly ducking back into his suite. Something seemed off. He looked like he was hiding something. (What I didn't know was that Brad had flown my father in for the day so he, in person and off camera, could ask for Dad's blessing to marry me.)

For the next few hours, as I was getting ready for the final rose ceremony, I had my picture taken a hundred different times in a hundred different ways doing a hundred different things.

"Emily, pick up your cup and look to the side."

"Emily, write in your journal."

"Emily, walk toward that palm tree and look pensive."

The show's stylist was back with a rack of dresses for me to choose, as was a makeup artist and a local hair stylist. When it was time to do my hair, I showed the woman a picture of what I wanted done. Simple beach waves. She nodded and proceeded to whip out a curling iron the size of a pencil. I gulped. I wasn't a professional hairdresser by any means, but I did know that particular piece of equipment wasn't meant to create beach waves, more like orphan Annie ringlets. I kept my mouth shut though. She was the professional, not me. When thirty minutes of curling had passed, my producer, who was hanging out with me, cocked his head and asked, "Um, is Emily's hair supposed to look like that?"

I jumped up from my chair, turning around to face the mirror, and started bawling. I looked like I had just stuck my finger in an electrical socket. I didn't have time to get in the shower and start over, so another stylist shuttled over and tried her best to mask what was now a brushed-out, brittle mess by straightening the heck out of my hair. It wasn't a good start to such an important day. Maybe even a bad sign.

I drove in a white Mercedes limousine to the winery where I would either get proposed to or dumped. My initial surety in being Brad's final pick waned. After last night's shenanigans, who knew what would happen? My producer and I drove for miles and miles down the interstate, passing through one shantytown after another. Staring at these dilapidated tin houses stacked on top of one another, as stable as a house of cards, gave me some perspective.

Here I was, driving in a luxury car, wearing a designer dress, just having had my hair done twice, on this successful TV show, having traveled to the most exotic places in the world. I couldn't help but think, *My word. I am so blessed.* A part of me felt guilty, almost foolish, for the opportunity I was given, while these beautiful South African people, and many more across the world, were living in absolute poverty. The tears fell, and my stomach twisted into a heavy knot.

As we pulled up a long, winding gravel road, I started getting nauseated. I didn't feel well at all. Chris Harrison greeted me as I got out of the limo. I tried to read his face, hoping I could gauge either a hint of sympathy or excitement, some telltale sign of what I could expect. Nothing. We weren't able to talk as we were filmed walking down a long pathway framed by enormous granite boulders and translucent ponds showing off brightly colored koi fish.

After crossing through a large room in the winery, Chris and I stood at the top of steep stairs that would lead me down yet another path where Brad would be waiting. Chris wished me luck, and I oh so carefully took step after step down that staircase, praying I wouldn't fall.

By the time I set foot on solid ground, I was able to look up and around, soaking in the stunning scenery of luscious green meadows and gorgeous mountain views. And there Brad was. As I stepped closer, I tried to read him. *Does he look happy? Worried? Like he's been crying?* I couldn't tell.

I stood before him, overwhelmed, a bit scared. It felt like an out-of-body experience, like I was hovering above, watching the spectacle, almost detached. After Brad offered a romantic monologue of his feelings for me, he said, "Please let me be your best friend. Please let me protect you and your beautiful daughter. And please give me the opportunity to love you for the rest of your life. I love you, Emily."

Then, Brad got down on one knee and popped the question. The proposal was quiet. No dramatic music played (it is not as theatrical as what you see on TV), and no one on the set barely even moved an inch, let alone said a word. It was strange.

As I said before, in hindsight, my feelings were muddled by many different variables. Obviously I liked the guy. And obviously I wanted to get to know him better. But I couldn't say I loved him. And while at the time I said I was falling in love with him—and on the episode you hear all the sound bites to that effect—I don't know how true that was. Yes, I was looking for love. Yes, I wanted to fall in love so desperately. And yes, I wanted to want to marry the guy. But it was all so premature. I wasn't ready to start a life with someone. As I said before, I had no business being engaged. When I look back at the video of that day, I hardly recognize myself. I don't even connect with that person.

After I said yes, Brad scooped me up in his arms and said, "Wow, Em! You're a lot heavier than you look." Well, that about ruined the tender moment. He knew my weight had always been a sore spot. Noticing his comment bothered me,

Brad issued a quick, "Oh, I was just kidding." You can see why this never aired. Very unromantic.

Almost immediately after the yes, the glamour and glitz and fairy tale and all the rest of the glittery-but-not-really-gold stuff was pretty much over. It seemed like someone had bellowed, "It's a wrap, people!" Literally, the minute after I said, "I do," all the camera equipment was shut off and started getting packed up, lighting was being broken down, and the producers and other staff on the show started making their way out of the winery. Crazy, right? There is no smooth transition back into reality. Chris Harrison didn't guide us back into the real world with words of wisdom. No network counselor came to talk to us about what happens next. Brad and I were pretty much on our own to venture into a new version of real life.

We spent the next few days together at his suite. We couldn't go anywhere because the paparazzi had somehow managed to snap some pictures of us together, so it was back to confinement. We didn't do much of anything other than lay out by the pool, being polite to each other. The fact was, I hardly knew the guy. Oh sure, we both had experienced an intense two months, but we hardly had an actual relationship. It was almost like hanging out with a stranger, definitely not a fiancé.

When I think back, I remember hoping my feelings would grow stronger. I did love the idea of being together with someone, but something was missing. Oh, Brad and I snuggled and cuddled and all that jazz, but I wouldn't say we had fun. You know, the kind of fun where you can laugh and joke and be silly and comfortable. Though we had some connection, of course, our time together was quiet, awkward, maybe even bland at times. I thought maybe it was normal, given the circumstances, and he and I just needed more time off camera to unwind and resettle into somewhat of a normalcy.

A few days later, Brad flew back to Austin. And I, without a Neil Lane diamond ring sparkling on my left hand, journeyed back home. I couldn't wear the ring at this time, so a producer took it back with her.

nine

It was a few weeks before November 2010 when I settled into a new and at times very emotionally draining normal. I was engaged to be married. It didn't quite sink in, so I let myself float about the strange reality. Also, I didn't give Ricki the full scoop when I got back. It's not as though Brad and I had set a date; we were both very aware we needed time.

Because the show wasn't going to air until January, Brad and I had to keep our relationship under wraps until the season finale in March. Which meant many phone calls, exchanges of cute care packages and cards, and several secret get-togethers in Los Angeles where we would stay in an undisclosed location courtesy of the network. Brad and I went incognito during those visits. Flying separately, of course, and staying put in the house so no one would know we were together.

I remember my first flight out to see Brad. Because we'd be homebound, I packed only the essentials, particularly loungewear. Lots of leggings and my cozy UGG boots. I was thankful this was one time I didn't need to pack a gown or be strategic in my wardrobe. When we'd wake up in the morning, I'd basically stay put in my comfies, but Brad would get decked out, wearing designer jeans, a nice shirt, and dressy shoes. So while I spent our time together looking relatively homeless, Brad looked like he was going out to eat at a trendy hotspot. Not a very warm and cozy match.

Things between us were tough during that time, definitely not lovey-dovey. So much so that a few weeks after we filmed the last show, Brad sent an e-mail, copying me, to the producers saying, *Sorry but things didn't work out with Emily and I. It wasn't the fairy tale I thought it would be.* That was the first of a hundred breakups. While I wasn't surprised by what Brad wrote—I mean, really, he was right—I was surprised to hear this from him via a cc on an e-mail.

One of the producers I had become good friends with called me and said, "Hey, what's up? What's going on between you and Brad?"

"I have no idea," was my reply.

Soon after, Brad and I got back together, me willing to give our relationship another shot. Look, I wasn't perfect. Brad wasn't the sole cause of our friction. I had my own share of insecurities and emotional baggage that interfered with what I hoped would have been a healthy relationship. Clearly, I wasn't ready. But I kept trying to make it work. We both did. In our own unhealthy ways. In hindsight, this wasn't a cause either one of us should have fought so hard for.

Brad and I continued to talk before the show aired in January and did a great job of keeping everything hush-hush. There were rumors going around online that Brad had dumped me, chosen Chantal, and spent Thanksgiving with her in Seattle. I can't tell you how many people approached me around town who had gobbled up that false information.

Whether I was grabbing a coffee at Starbucks or checking out groceries at the supermarket, strangers would come up to me, with maudlin eyes and big sighs, and say, "Oh honey, I'm so sorry you didn't end up with Brad. It's for the best" or, "I'm sorry it didn't work out, but I'll bet you'll make a great Bachelorette!" And because I wasn't allowed to say one word in response, I'd just politely smile and nod.

Things really heated up in January, and not in a good way. Brad and I had been fighting a lot over the phone. About stupid things. Half of them I can't even remember. And once the show aired, my relatively quiet life in Charlotte ended. I had this huge secret that everyone wanted to know (who did Brad pick?) and that everyone was asking me about, from paparazzi that hounded me outside my house, waiting for me to leave so they could follow me, to friends and family who swore if I told them who Brad picked, they wouldn't say a word to anyone. But I had signed a bulletproof contract and kept quiet. Well, not entirely. The only person I told was my mother. Hey, it was my mother, for Pete's sake! And I know for a fact she didn't tell a soul.

Staying quiet proved a difficult task once I started getting beat up in the media. One magazine accused me of being obsessed with plastic surgery. Another announced I was not a nice person. One website declared me a jealous nut. Another labeled me a bad mom. That last one killed me. I may not pride myself on a ton of things, but I do on being a great mom. That bold-faced gossip was a low blow and put me in a really depressed mood.

Having to constantly battle paparazzi just about put me over the edge. It was annoying to drive to the grocery store with Ricki and, as soon as we hopped out of the car, be assaulted by a handful of guys with their bulky cameras asking me a million questions, none of which, of course, I could answer. I will say that some paps were respectful and tried to give me space, especially if I was out with Ricki, who ate up every bit of the attention. But some weren't so nice. I tried to be polite, but after a while I was dangerously close to, ahem, "going crosses" on them.

Instead of giving the media more material to write negative stories about me, I became a recluse. Outside of taking Ricki to and from school and her activities, I stayed home. If I wasn't out and about, nobody could bother me. What was supposed to be the highlight of my life was turning out to be a really lonely time. The alienation was burdensome, digging my depression deeper, though I was committed to putting on a happy face for the sake of my daughter.

As time passed, Brad and I spent more time fighting than relating. We watched the show separately and even though it was in the past, seeing his relationship progress with Chantal on camera felt like a punch to my gut. Some of the things he said to her, he had said to me. I also noticed he was more physically attentive to her, which hurt. Right before each episode aired, I felt sick to my stomach wondering what else would shock me about the two of them.

When Brad and I were about to film the *After the Final Rose* episode with Chris Harrison, needless to say we weren't so enthusiastic. The producers didn't seem too worried by our rocky road and told us to be honest, to explain that neither we nor our relationship was perfect. *Great!* I thought. *No need to put on a front.* I took the producer's guidance as an open door to be transparent. The problem was, it was daunting to sit on a stage in front of hundreds of people (believe it or not, it's very different than being filmed on the show for two-plus months), and before taking my seat with Brad and Chris, I had drunk some alcohol in the greenroom.

So, thanks to my indulgence of liquid courage, what I thought was me being transparent about our relationship was, well, perhaps a little too much and not very respectful. Brad only talked about how great things were between us and how much he adored me. I, however, flavored my affection for him with the hard truth, in so many words, that this wasn't a perfect match. There were some things I said that at the time I imagine painted me as a stand-up comedian, but when I watched the show later, looking at Brad's face in response, I realized I wasn't being funny or nice. And I'm sorry for that.

I flew out to Austin in March 2011 so Brad and I could watch the season finale and *After the Final Rose* together. Talk about spoiler alert—I still can't believe the network let us do that. In the airport, I passed by fellow travelers who said, "Well, I guess we know who won!"

That weekend finally felt right. It was light, fun. Exactly what Brad and I needed. We went shopping. I met his friends. We hung out at SXSW and listened to awesome music. We had even talked about me moving to Austin. But when we watched the *After the Final Rose* episode right after the season finale, Brad let me know clear as day how upset he was over my antics. It was not a fun moment for us. But even though things between us weren't the perfect shade of peachy, I was still convinced that all we needed was more time. Once the weight of not being able to talk to anyone about our experience was lifted, I was confident the state of our relationship would improve.

But I was wrong.

Though Brad knew I was a Christian and we went to church together the few times he came to Charlotte and even when I visited him in Austin, I didn't realize at the time how important it was to find someone with a strong faith. A part of me thought that maybe I could influence him to follow Christ, which in hindsight was pretty silly because my faith was mediocre, lukewarm, not something my life was centered on. Maybe if we both deepened our spiritual lives, things would improve. It was almost a shallow thought, however, because my relationship with God wasn't much of a priority.

When I came back to Charlotte after that great weekend in March, the fighting picked up right where it left off. My whole mood was dependent on what was happening between Brad and me. If things were good, I felt like the queen of the world. And when they weren't, I quickly plummeted down into the dumps.

Not long after, Brad and I broke up, for good this time. When the media firestorm broke out speculating the end of our relationship, the network asked me to do an interview with Chris Harrison to finally put the rumors to rest.

I wish I'd said no. I wish I cared less what others thought and more about what God thought. I should have refocused my priorities, remembering and relying more on my faith, which was totally on the back burner at this point. I'm embarrassed to say this, but I had turned the show, even Brad, into an idol. I spent more time Googling my name, to see what hurtful things were being said about me, than doing what I should have been doing, namely studying the Word of God, soaking in what He, not others, says about me.

The interview was horrible. All I did was cry. I cried as soon as I pulled into the Bachelor mansion. I cried as soon as I saw familiar producers. I cried when I saw Chris. I cried because the last time I had walked into this beautiful house, I was hopeful I was going to find love. And then I was hopeful that things would get better between Brad and me. But the hope I kept on building and building was unsustainable. As I sat down with Chris, who was very sympathetic, and cameras angled their way on me, I felt like a failure. A failure and incredibly lonely. I tried so hard not to cry ugly, but all these emotions were gushing out of me. I don't think every tear had to do with Brad. I think a lot of it came from my disappointment of taking a chance at love and falling flat on my face. In front of millions and millions of people. How embarrassing!

Some people may think, *Well, you asked for it, so you deserve the media whipping, the embarrassment—all those things.* I can't tell you how many people have accused me of going on the show to become famous. While hindsight is always 20/20, I will say this: While I didn't say yes to *The Bachelor* because I wanted to bask in the C-list limelight, at the time I felt something in my life was missing. And I thought that being on the show might fill that void, whatever it was. I'll also say that once that C-list fame came tumbling toward me, I didn't want any part of it. I'm not trying to defend myself, but I think my actions speak for themselves. Brad and I didn't do many post-show interviews, and I shied away from the parties, the red carpet events, and the idea of moving to Los Angeles. I'm not saying my intentions were 100 percent pure—the Bible does say our hearts are deceitful little things—but I think if I wanted fame, I would have done more things to hold on stronger to the attention.

Producers had asked me if I'd consider being a Bachelorette on season 7. My response? "Thank you, but absolutely not!" (I was so happy to hear that Ashley H. had signed up for that season, and I wished her all the best!) It was neat to be offered the opportunity, but I wanted a normal life, a life absent of media hounding me and having my love life dissected by the American population. And when I finally told Chris Harrison, and the world, that I was single again, that's what happened. Normal. I became old news. The paparazzi mellowed out and eventually moved out of my neighborhood. The tabloids stopped including me in their stories. Frankly, I felt relieved.

But while I had my privacy back for the most part, something in me had changed. I had become more guarded. I didn't trust many people, so it was hard to have authentic friendships. I became paranoid, wondering who was genuine and who wasn't. I'm sure I prematurely burned some bridges during this time, but I was so on edge, I didn't know what to do. Or think. So I remained lonely. And in many ways, empty.

In my search to find meaning and fulfillment, I started attending a new church in town, Forest Hill. I was surprised by how warm and welcoming everyone was, an inviting change from what I had experienced in the tabloids. I even started volunteering there. The church had adopted an elementary school down the road and gave students the opportunity to join neat extracurricular clubs (athletics, crafts, arts). Forest Hill was looking for group leaders to run some of these clubs, so I volunteered to lead the jewelry one. Every Thursday, Ricki and I would pack up boxes of beads, string, and other supplies and spend an hour or two with twenty girls and boys, teaching them how to make cool necklaces and bracelets. The kids were loud and goofy and an absolute joy to be around. I loved it. Ricki did too.

The first week I signed up as a group leader, our church hosted a big event in the school auditorium, where all the students gathered and the group leaders explained the different clubs that were available. I stood in the middle of the gym floor with the other leaders, waiting for the mic to make its round so I could offer my spiel. One of the leaders before me, this guy named Tyler, introduced himself and his club. I had seen him around church and knew he was an elder. He was very hard to miss because he was so, um, hot!

Tyler was tall, muscular, and super confident. Because he was so good-looking, and a church leader, I assumed he was either weird or boring. I later told someone in my small group that Tyler was the most beautiful man I'd ever met. But my admiration got quickly shut down when the person said something about him having a girlfriend. Oh well.

But every Thursday for the next few months after Jewelry Club, Tyler would help me carry my boxes of beads and such from the school to my car. We small-talked and developed a friendship. One evening, as he shoved the last box of crystals into the trunk of my car, he mentioned that his brother had recently asked him if he knew the girl from Charlotte who was just on *The Bachelor*. Never having watched the show before,

Tyler told his brother he didn't. His brother then told him he should because he had a feeling Tyler was going to marry her. Well, that was a first! I'd never before heard such a bold pickup line, if that's what it was.

I got all shaky and sweaty and giggled politely in response. I didn't know what to say, oh, except give him my number, with Ricki in the background playfully repeating each digit I spoke. While Tyler has a different take on what exactly happened around this time, I recall him calling or texting me a few times and me not responding in typical unsure-afraid Emily fashion. Don't even ask why I probably came across as standoffish because I couldn't even give you a straight answer if I wanted to. I think maybe, even after he asked for my number, I was strictly in the friend zone, as there had never been any kind of romantic talk or flirtations between the two of us.

Sometime after Halloween 2011, the producers of *The Bachelorette* flew down to Charlotte to try and convince me to do the show. Ashley's season had finished airing and Ben Flajnik was the current Bachelor. I appreciated their valiant efforts (boy, these guys were persistent), but I said no. I wasn't ready. And I didn't have a peace about it. But as weeks passed and my loneliness grew, I started reconsidering. I don't know if it was time, or being in denial, or curiosity, or what, but I felt—please, please, please don't laugh or roll your eyes—that if God had closed the door with Brad maybe He was beside this open door, beckoning me in. Maybe this was my real chance at falling in love.

So I said yes. For the second time.

A week or two before I was scheduled to fly out to Los Angeles, Tyler and I were walking back to the car after our school clubs one Thursday night when I told him I was going on the show. He seemed taken aback. Before I drove off, Tyler said something like, "Well, let's keep in touch as friends then, and if you're not engaged when you get back, we can get together or something."

I went on the show with pure intentions. I truly did want to meet my husband, not necessarily get engaged but find someone who I could, one day, see the possibility of marrying. I wanted to prove everyone wrong and show the world that I could find love, that it could happen, even on something as silly as a TV show. I wanted to be the poster child for a love success story. Most important, I trusted the peace I had, this strong feeling that prompted me to make the decision.

I knew that peace couldn't come from the devil, so I assumed it was from God and that it was an internal sign of Him blessing my decision. And I figured if I had such a peace, something good was going to happen. Surely God wouldn't put me at ease only to watch me fall flat on my face in heartbreak . . . on national TV . . . again. Right? Now, all that being said, was I confident I would, in fact, find my husband? Not really. But I was super hopeful I would.

When I told my mom my decision to be the next Bachelorette, she laughed. "Emily, I just don't understand." Still, Mom was as supportive as ever. She may have voiced her concerns, but she always stood beside me with all my crazy ideas. I have always valued her consistent presence and that she never gave up on me.

And I'm sure Mom felt a little more confident this time around that I wouldn't make a total fool out of myself on national TV. I'm sure she was just hoping I'd find love by the more traditional route.

I told the producers I'd do the show under one condition—Ricki would be with me this time. (I would tell her, as I did the last time, that I was hosting a show, not being on a show to find love.)

Mom was also able to accompany me some of the time. I was thrilled to be able to share these memories with her. And I know part of her being close to me and involved in the process made her feel more comfortable about what I was doing. Oh yeah, one more important thing. I was adamant with the producers about the fact that I did not want to get engaged on the show. I was hoping for love, not a fiancé. From what I remember, the producers got my drift. Or so I thought.

The ground rules were the same for the most part. I was sworn to secrecy during filming and for a time after and could have no contact with the outside world via phone, computer, or Internet during the process. Also, because I'd been on *The Bachelor*, I had a pretty good idea of how things were run on the show and what I could expect. Now, while not every single thing is scripted, I was well aware that there would be plenty of times I'd have to follow specific direction from the producers.

In the beginning of February 2012, right around my twenty-sixth birthday, I went to Los Angeles to finalize the arrangements and—one of the best parts—choose my wardrobe! I was assigned two producers who would be by my side throughout the entire journey, yes, even on my dates. One was a free-spirited and laid-back surfer chick with long blonde hair. She didn't care what anyone thought of her and took every opportunity to act goofy and make me laugh when I was in a bad mood. She had a particular talent for dancing like a goofball and whipping her hair around to the beat of Jersey Shore–worthy club music, something she did often to cheer me up.

The other, a hippie chick, just got me. She knew when to give me space and when, and how hard, to push my buttons. The three of us had a great time together. We laughed together. We cried together. And though we bonded like sisters, our time wasn't without some hiccups (more on that later).

Together the three of us rummaged through the racks and racks of amazing clothes that the show's stylist had carefully laid out for me in his minimalist yet very chic condo. Oh my goodness, I was in heaven, surrounded by beautiful fabrics and exquisite designs, clothes I'd only dreamed of wearing.

As my producers picked up a string of stunning ball gowns, bikinis, blouses, and shorts, they'd whisper to one another, pointing to a particular article of clothing, "Oh, that would be perfect for such-and-such." They knew my entire schedule, and while I was only privy to the fact that we'd be filming in Charlotte for a while, I had no idea where we'd be taken or what we'd do outside of North Carolina. Boy, I loved surprises! And being surprised as the Bachelorette was much more fun than being surprised when you're just one out of thirty girls.

I started getting worked up, in a good way, when I was in Los Angeles. Oh sure, a few nerves were present (I wouldn't be Emily Maynard without them), but this time around I actually felt that I was on a fun adventure. And that was more confidence-inspiring than trying to connect with a guy alongside so many women who were trying to do the same.

At the beginning of March, a week before we started filming, the network shipped to my house all the necessary equipment and props, which a crew member stacked and stored using every inch of space in my garage. I have never seen so many different kinds of cameras, lighting equipment, microphone packs, and (can't forget the favorite prop) candles in my entire life! When it came time to set up my house for taping, the crew worked so hard and did an amazing job not to make a total disruptive mess of cable and wires. This was especially important because at times my house looked like a kids' club. What was so neat about this experience was that many of the producers (and even Chris Harrison at one point) brought their kids along with them. I love the sound of a house full of kid giggles and chatter. And Ricki? Well, she was over the moon at having some playmates around.

We filmed around town the first few days. Ricki and I had a few photo shoots together, and I did a few solo interviews at home and at various locations around our neighborhood. I followed the producers' leads to "Push Ricki on the swing" and "Run with the balloons in your hand, then let them go" and "Crawl into bed and start writing in your journal." It was basically a lot of direction and a lot of filming. My little girl and I had a blast. She loved the attention, the whirlwind of excitement that comes with being filmed and surrounded by a crew of people.

I vowed to myself that things would be different this time. On *The Bachelor*, I was guarded, reserved. On *The Bachelorette*, I made a commitment to put myself out there and bare my soul. I knew these producers were screening men left and right to find me great matches, and part of my being vulnerable and transparent was a testament that I believed they could help me find love.

I started getting ready for the initial meet and greet at three in the afternoon in the comfort of my own home. I can't tell you how good it felt to be there and not some strange hotel. The guys were staying in a gorgeous rented mansion fifteen minutes away, where in only a couple of hours they'd introduce themselves to me, mingle at the cocktail party, and—eek!—participate in their first rose ceremony.

In the early evening, my producers and I left my house to head toward the Bachelorette mansion, where I'd temporarily occupy the master bedroom for the final touches on my makeup and hair. We listened to a local radio station as we rode. When Jay-Z's song "Forever Young" came on, I rolled the window down and stuck my hand out, waving it in sync with the beat. Gratitude washed over me. I couldn't believe so many people, the producers, the cameramen, the stylists, the staff, and everyone involved in this process, had taken time out of their lives to come to Charlotte and help me find love. It was humbling to even think about.

While I was having this moment, one of my producers looked at me and rolled her eyes in her imitable way. "For Pete's sake, Emily, are you crying?"

I smiled and started laughing. "This whole thing is crazy. Good crazy!" I replied. (Note I said "good" crazy, not weird crazy like meeting a bachelor and his ostrich egg, but I'm getting way ahead of myself here.)

Chris Harrison was waiting for me at the mansion. He was great, very funny. I got to know him a bit better this time around, though I didn't spend time with him off camera talking about the guys or my experience. That sort of chitchat was reserved for my producers.

The twenty-five bachelors hadn't piled in by the time I arrived, so I took a brief tour of the place, walking past thousands of flickering candles large and small and admiring the breathtaking home. My producers talked me through the night so I knew what was going to happen. It was pretty simple. Meet some guys, take breaks for interviews, meet more guys, break for more interviews, welcome all the guys at the cocktail party, talk to some one-on-one, take a break for another set of interviews, more guys, more interviews, and finally the first rose ceremony, where I'd have to say good-bye to five guys.

Ah, the dreaded rejection drama. That day, feeling a very bold and confident self, I was sure I'd have no trouble sending guys home right and left. Oh, sure. This is so easy to say when you are not the one rejecting the guy face-to-face and in front of millions of people.

When the sun slipped past the horizon, I knew what time it was. I was ready, so ready, to meet these eligible bachelors! My producers positioned me on a literal X by the front door of the house, where I was to wait for the boys to roll in. It was important to stay on that exact spot facing a certain way. If any guy would compromise that position, I'd have to, as smoothly as possible, scoot him over. Before my producers left my side, they told me to have fun. Oh boy.

Sean stepped out of the first limo, all-American, big muscles, warm eyes, and a kind smile. I was off to a great start. Because I knew how nerve-wracking it could be to stand in their shoes, I did my best to make the guys feel comfortable. After Sean, the trail of cute boys continued along with my giving the producers a thumbs-up or thumbs-down sign after they walked off and into the house. I was so giddy that the meet and greet was a blur.

Some of the entry stunts were definitely entertaining (e.g., Mrs. Doubtfire guy, boom-box Jersey guy). Some were cute, like Jef gliding on his skateboard. And some were just odd, enter the ostrich egg–toting guy. I remember standing and kind of waiting, or hoping, that maybe someone was going to step out of a limo and I would just know beyond a shadow of a doubt that he was the one, my future husband. But that never happened.

When that phase of the evening was done, I had to pick the guys I liked and which I didn't. It was so hard to say because I couldn't remember all of them. Wait. Of course I remembered Kalon flying down in the helicopter, but not for good reason. I wasn't impressed by his showy entrance. It was a tacky, off-putting gimmick that came across as pretentious.

Meeting these potential mates took place within only a minute or two, so it was hard, almost impossible, to find a connection or remember the guys vividly before they were whisked off. I did my best. While being on *The Bachelor* was a waiting game, being a Bachelorette was nonstop. I learned this immediately. There was no downtime.

I welcomed the guys at the beginning of the cocktail party, making sure I hit the one or two points the producers suggested I mention but mainly sticking to my own heartfelt thoughts. And then, it was time to get to know the guys. Producers scurried off to find me particular bachelors to talk to. None of them could approach me without permission, so it's more orchestrated than it looks on TV. But think about it, and not just in my case. Imagine the chaos of guys and girls clamoring over the Bachelorette or Bachelor had producers not guided the whole thing. Madness, right?

I could write that it was exhausting, or that I didn't enjoy the constant motion, or that I felt like a piece of meat meeting all these guys, but I'd be lying. It was fun. Really fun! When was I ever going to have the chance to meet so many potential significant others in one place? Um, never. For real this time.

Some guys were nice. Some were funny. Some were cute. Some were intense, purging their emotional baggage over me. And some stood before me in awkward silence, not knowing what to say as I desperately tried to fill the wordless gap by asking them get-to-know-you questions. When it was time to wrap up whatever conversation I was in, producers would give me a signal, and I'd—sometimes smoothly, sometimes painfully—say some form of, "Well, thank you for chatting with me. I'll look for you later tonight." And then it was time to move on to the next guy. Phew!

I gave Doug the first impression rose. He had read me the cutest letter from his son. I bonded with him being a single parent and all. The producers thought he was a great first pick, not just because he had a child but because he was likely the least threatening to the other guys.

I will say the guy who stood out the most was smoldering Arie. We had the strongest connection and he knew how to make me laugh, which was definitely a plus! I don't remember much of what we talked about because I was so nervous, but I liked his whole vibe. When he told me he was a race-car driver, my first, somewhat disappointing thought was, *Oh, great. So that's why you're on the show.*

A part of me felt like it was a setup, as if the producers

hoped I'd pick him and create this redemption-like fairy-tale love story. Something along the lines of getting back what I lost so many years ago. I tried not to let those thoughts distract me, however, because I wanted to stay present with Arie. And I also had to start thinking about which five guys to send home. And I didn't know! I didn't even have a clue how to begin weeding them out.

After the rose ceremony, I had to do one more interview before I could head home. It was about eight in the morning the next day by the time I pulled into my driveway. I slept for a bit and had the rest of the day off. Ricki and I spent the day together, getting our nails done at the house (thank you, ABC!) and watching movies. My producers came over later, and over sushi, the three of us gabbed about the remaining twenty guys.

During filming, they had notebooks where they jotted down comments, ideas, and future to-do's. In the back, they had written down after that first rose ceremony their guesses at whom I would pick at the final one. They shared this with me when the show was over, and we all had a big laugh at their choices. One of my producers had picked Ryan, Jesus-football guy (he's coming right up), and the other had chosen Alessandro, the vampire hunter (who I'll get to in the next chapter). I couldn't believe they were so off. But hey, this just proves that first impressions and gut calls aren't all that matter.

My first date, which was arranged for the next day, was with Ryan. I'll say, at least at first, it was the perfect choice because he was very easygoing and talked a lot, which took a lot of pressure off me.

After packing Ricki's lunch and dropping her off at school, I picked Ryan up at the Bachelorette mansion. Then it was back to my house where we made cookies for Ricki's soccer team. It was very amusing to watch this good-looking, burly guy don an apron and mix batter. But after a while, the cute factor wore off because it seemed he only talked about two things: Jesus and football. Now, I love me some Jesus talk, but that doesn't mean I necessarily want to get preached to on a first date. And football? Well, you know how much I'm into sports. During the date, I had to take the occasional break to film an interview, and I ended up intentionally leaving the kitchen every few minutes to ask the producers for help.

"There's too much Jesus and football talk!" I told my producers. "Can't you guys do anything?" Pulling up to dinner later that night and being greeted by what looked to me like half of Charlotte, as well as dancing in front of them while one of my favorite bands, Gloriana, played in the background, was pretty crazy, but cool. And even though Ryan continued to gab, I kept him around. Every guy deserves a chance, right?

The group date the next day involved hanging out with the Muppets, which was mind-blowing. I grew up watching the show, and here was Kermit, zipping up my dress, making Miss Piggy jealous. I got to bring my mom and Ricki backstage with me and was so grateful I could share this amazing experience with them. The day was awesome, even though the producers and I had a bit of an argument because they wanted me to sing the song "Rainbow Connection," and I, who can't carry a tune to save my life, was not going to belt out this famous song on national TV. I'll never forget calling Ricki, who was in the audience, to join me on stage for the duet with Kermit. I'd never seen her run so fast in her life. And the entire time, her eyes were wide with awe.

By the end of the night I felt more tired than I ever had. It wasn't just a physical tired; it was a mental drain. Not wanting to be a dud, I pushed through the exhaustion. I gave a rose to one-F Jef during this episode, even though he was aloof and it looked like he was running away from me one time. I saw so much of myself, when I was on *The Bachelor*, in him, and I wanted to give him the confidence that Brad had always gone out of his way to give me.

I did, however, say good-bye to Joe that same episode. I can't tell you how uncomfortable I felt having to reject him on camera. He didn't do anything wrong; I just didn't feel a connection. And while the process of sending bachelors home never got easier, especially because I was sure the families and friends of all those men would hate me, after a while I knew they'd be more than fine. And I'm sure some of the guys were happy to go home. I wasn't going to flatter myself and think I was the girl of every bachelor's dream and that they'd be crushed to pieces when they didn't receive a rose. I'm pretty charming, but I certainly don't think that highly of myself. Besides, I knew there was a long line of girls waiting for them at home just because they had been on the show. Later that night, Aaron and Kyle went home as well.

I went to bed, as I would continue to do throughout filming, around three or four in the morning. Those were some long days! I prayed more during this time, hoping I was honoring God the best way I could, given the circumstances. My feelings started to get a little conflicted at this point. Now, don't get me wrong. I was having a blast, fun, lots of fun. But I wondered if this really was God's plan for my life.

Was part of His purpose for me getting to go on a million

dates one after another and (eventually) making out with some of the guys? Was the Holy Spirit really guiding me, or was my heart being led more by what I wanted? This would continue to be an internal struggle, even in the midst of my gallivanting. I couldn't shake the peace I had felt when I opted to do the show, but when the process was underway, I couldn't shake the questions—some that never stopped coming.

ten

I smiled like a giddy schoolgirl when I knew that Arie was going to be my third one-on-one date. Since the first day we met, I felt attracted to his smoky, sweet self. While some of my dates or conversations with some of the bachelors flopped miserably, during which I'd practically beg the producers for some direction or guidance so we wouldn't stay stuck in silence, I'd never experienced anything like that with Arie. Our conversations had always flowed naturally, with ease. The producers arranged for us to spend the day at Dollywood, the greatest amusement park on earth as far as I'm concerned. It was the perfect setup all around for a great date.

But something in the air was off-kilter. I had asked him some questions and noticed his responses seemed defensive, like he was hiding something. I started entertaining crazy notions in my head but quickly turned that tape off. When Arie and I headed to the theater and one of my favorites, Dolly Parton, showed up, I could have died on the spot and been a very happy woman. Meeting the country legend was beyond words, as was my first kiss with Arie, which left quite an impression.

The pre–rose ceremony cocktail party later that night

started out okay, but got progressively worse. Travis took me outside to say good-bye to Shelly, the ostrich egg that I unapologetically smashed on the cobblestone driveway (it felt really good!). I spent a few minutes with Kalon, which affirmed his pretentious and condescending attitude. The moment he said, "I love to hear you talk, but only when I'm finished," I knew I didn't like him. At all. It was obvious Kalon wasn't winning any of the other guys over, and I knew it was a matter of time before he would dig his own grave by doing or saying something stupid. Besides, can you imagine how boring the show would be if I only kept the nice guys around the whole time?

Then came the Alessandro debacle. If you watched the show, you know I almost bowled over in shock when he associated my having a daughter as a compromise, the admission prompting me to send him home. But there was more to the guy than what aired. Alessandro, with I'm sure some inspiration from the producers, took things to a whole other level of crazy in a scene that never aired. After he informed me he was a vampire detector and suggested there was a vampire in the house, he then asked me to join him in the woods, which explains my combat boots as I walked out of the house.

Alessandro was babbling on about something, but I couldn't hear a word that was coming out of his mouth because my eyes were glued to these various-sized crosses that hung down from almost every limb on almost every tree. If the atmosphere wasn't creepy enough, I could see a fog machine in action vomiting a continual stream of haze around where we stood. While I was paralyzed in shock, the guy continued his disturbing vampire rant, none of which made any sense to me.

I knew in that moment that this particular bachelor and I lived on completely different planets.

The more he talked and the more dangling crosses I saw, the more furious I became. I don't know if the producers were trying to find a connection between my faith and Alessandro's, but I found the whole shenanigan utterly disrespectful. Sorry, folks, but I don't think Jesus has much in common with vampires. I was so angry, I remember hurling down the lantern I was carrying and yelling.

The producers actually shut down production for a bit because I was so mad. Later, Chris Harrison, who heard my outburst, told me, "I didn't know you had it in you to yell like that, Emily, but I loved it!" Perhaps I went a bit overboard, but I did not like being manipulated, which is exactly what I felt had happened. Eventually the tension died down, of course, and the producers and I had a good laugh over the fiasco; they affectionately christened my gust of fury as "going crosses."

The real speech I gave before the rose ceremony didn't air. I guess my words still betrayed much of the rage I felt. Part of what I really said to the well-dressed bachelors was, "I'm tired of vampire talk. This whole thing is starting to be a joke. I'm sorry you guys have to go through this, and though we're in it together, at this point I don't feel like I'm going to fall in love. This is too much." What aired, of course, was a much more generic, nonthreatening speech. I sent Stevie home that night and, of course, Alessandro. I should mention I had said goodbye to Tony earlier in the day. He was so distraught over missing his little boy. As a single mother, my heart reached out to him, and I couldn't in good conscience keep him on the show.

While it's exciting to be wooed by a slew of dreamy guys, I didn't want to get myself in the same situation as I did with Brad. I really had to get to know these guys, which was obviously pretty tough when there were so many of them. But I was committed to doing my best, which meant kissing some princes and sending home some frogs.

When the producers told me we were traveling to colorful Bermuda after Charlotte, I was ready to get my sun on with the thirteen remaining bachelors. For the rest of the six-week journey (good golly, as I write the words *six-week journey*, all I can think about is how short that really is to expect to find the love of your life!), I didn't know where I was going. Every trip was a surprise. I loved that! It felt like being a kid at Christmas, getting to rip into a new package every week.

Unfortunately, the weather in Bermuda was disappointing. I expected eighty degrees of hot sun, but my reality was a frigid fifty-degree couple of days. But you wouldn't have known that, watching the show. I still had to gallivant around in bikinis, tanks, and cutoff shorts, acting as if I were baking in the tropical heat.

Aside from the cold weather, the island itself was beautiful, from the jeweled sea to the pink sandy beaches to the charming shops around town.

Probably the most uncomfortable part of the trip was the two-on-one date where I was sandwiched awkwardly between John and Nate. I don't know anyone in the history of the show who hasn't felt weird, almost unnatural, on these kinds of dates. I, for one, felt like a dirty old man. Cliff diving was one activity on our itinerary. I think the show loves to have people jump off high places just as much as they love using candles as props! I was terrified at taking the plunge into the sparkling ocean. You already know adventure is not my thing. Now add jumping into freezing cold water to the list.

When I watched the show later, I laughed at how fired up I looked, taking this "leap of faith." Oh, and I couldn't help but laugh at what John said in the interview right before the clip of the three of us jumping into the water: "This could be a jumping-off point for the both of us." Why do I get the stinking feeling whoever was interviewing him asked him to compare that jump to our potential relationship? Oh yeah, now I remember. It's probably because that's exactly what happened!

The water enveloped me like a million knives slicing my skin. But that wasn't the worst part. As the guys were swimming off toward the boat, my body was in such shock from the cold temperature, I lost my ability to swim. I started panicking and flailing around like a floppy fish out of water until John swam back and rescued me. Not a very romantic moment, though I appreciated being saved from potentially drowning. Later that day, Nate made his way back home.

I started noticing Jef a lot in Bermuda. I liked the fact that he was quiet. While the other guys were a bit more aggressive, not holding back their feelings, Jef was more reserved. On that trip, I told one of my producers that I really liked him.

"Get to know him better," she suggested. Something in her voice implied a deeper meaning beyond her words. And by that time, I was very familiar with these kinds of intentionally probing conversations.

"Why?" I asked. "Is something wrong with him?"

"Just find out more," she said with a smile. "You know, about his family and stuff."

Ah. Clue number two. I didn't know at the time that she was referring to his Mormon background. But as my imagination started running wild, I thought to myself, *Oh great. I like the loser guy who still lives with his mother.* Of course, that ended up not being the case. I would eventually find out that while Jef's family members were devout in their religion, he didn't share those strong ties. He did, however, have so much knowledge about the Bible. This was something that impressed me, but also clouded my judgment. At one point after meeting his sweet and caring family, I wondered if Mormonism was a religion I could claim as my own. Ultimately, however, I didn't think much about how our different views on faith would mesh. Though I was a believer, I was spiritually dry and not understanding of how important faith ties are in a relationship.

Now that I've come out of that fog, I realize it's the foundation of a solid relationship.

After I made my decision of which two guys to send home while staring at the beautiful framed photographs of the remaining twelve guys, I started feeling miserable. Not just because I had to make tough choices but because the lack of sleep and unusually chilly weather had taken its toll on my body. I was feverish, shivering from body aches and nursing a wicked sore throat that took away my voice. But there was no time to chug some NyQuil and try to disappear in my bed.

The show wasn't just about me finding love. It was a job for the entire crew, producers, cameramen, and everyone in between. They all depended on me, so I sucked it up and pushed through, finishing off the evening with the final shots and interviews before collapsing in bed for a few hours. While I lay on my bed in a dazed stupor, the remaining bachelors—Doug,

Jef, John, Sean, Kalon, Alejandro, Arie, Travis, Chris, and Ryan—were packing for the next leg of this journey: London.

I'd never been to London before and I was so excited to go, downing loads of vitamin C to combat whatever illness I was suffering from. When producers shuffled me to the May Fair Hotel—a gorgeous boutique hotel that overlooked the hustle and bustle of the exclusive area of May Fair—I was a mess. I didn't get to do much oohing and ahhing before I plopped onto the plush bed, my ears in so much pain I was afraid they were going to burst. Concerned, the producers sent a doctor to my hot-pink hotel room. He diagnosed some kind of infection and gave me antibiotics that he promised would make me feel better soon.

London was chilly, more so than Bermuda, and the stylist who had helped plan out and pack my wardrobe for the next few weeks didn't bother to include a jacket. The last thing I wanted was to get sicker in this posh but very damp city, so my producers ran out and bought me a cashmere Burberry jacket. Not that I expected them to get me a puffy Starter jacket or anything, but the gesture was more than generous. (Note to self: get sick on every trip.)

That night my producers, noticing my Casper complexion, made an appointment for me to get a spray tan at a nearby salon. Once inside, it looked more like a creepy dungeon than a beauty shop. The service was as sketchy as the interior design. Let's just say I came out of there as orange as Ross from the episode of *Friends* in which he overdid his spray tan. Later, over a dimly lit dinner, my producers howled with laughter, barely getting out the words, "All we can see are your white teeth!" This time, I thanked my lucky stars for cold weather.

A perfect excuse to wear gloves and cover the botched job on my hands.

My first date in London was with Sean. I liked him, the all-American boy who was good-looking, super nice, athletic, and an overall good guy. He was a great, safe choice. I did worry, however, that if I ended up not picking him in the long run, all of America would hate me. While Sean was a great catch, there was still a bit of a disconnect. I wanted him to come out of his shell more. Maybe I was to blame. Maybe I didn't make him feel comfortable or didn't say the right things. The bottom line was, however, the chemistry just wasn't there.

April 2 was Ricky's birthday, which my daughter and I always celebrate by releasing a balloon. The producers let me have the morning off so Ricki and I could continue our tradition and spend quiet time together walking around magnificent London. I was in a funk the entire day, but appreciated the producers giving me space to do this off camera. They had asked if they could film some of our private moments, but I refused. Remembering my girl's daddy was reserved for us, off the record. And I didn't want to share it with anyone (sorry America!).

While London kicked off relatively drama-free, the upcoming group date was a breeding ground for an inevitable firestorm. I knew it would come sometime; I just didn't know how. The guys and I headed to a quaint English pub to sample some exotic brews. As Doug and I sipped on foamy beers, he said he wanted to talk to me about something and proceeded to inform me that sometime that day Kalon had referred to my beautiful daughter, Ricki, as "baggage."

After Doug spilled the beans, I sat on the couch fuming. I don't think he understood how mad I was. He tried to change the subject and cash in on some one-on-one time, but all I could think about was what Kalon had said. Say what you want about me, but don't you dare say a word about my little girl. And certainly don't be a coward and say it behind my back. I can't tell you how badly I wanted to go West Virginia Hood Rat Backwoods on Kalon. As furious as I was, I felt bad for his mom. As she, too, was a single mother, I could only imagine how embarrassed she would be at his comment when the episode aired.

When I walked into the room where all the guys were chilling on buttery leather couches, I felt like spewing venom. And I did. After I gave Kalon a verbal lashing, no one said a word. Everyone was as quiet as a church mouse. While I appreciated that Doug had given me the scoop, in that moment, I felt alone. Very alone. Here I was with a bunch of guys who were all saying they liked me, yet it seemed I was fighting this battle on my own. And so I left, walking out of the pub with a scowl on my face. To my disappointment, no one followed me. Another reminder that I was alone. I was most disappointed in Arie. He and I shared such a strong connection. And he clearly knew I was upset. I hoped at least he would step up on my behalf. But nope. I got zilch.

As I walked back to my hotel, my heels clomping loudly on the sidewalk, the damp air seeped into my skin. My mind reeled. I began to wonder if the lull in the room after I reamed out Kalon was because the other guys weren't so innocent. Maybe they had something to hide that Kalon could use as ammunition. Maybe if they tried to say anything in my defense, Kalon could have switched the attention on them and whatever hurtful or not-so-nice comment they might have said.

I cried the whole walk to the hotel, my eyes stinging, my shoulders heavy. I didn't just feel sick from the infection I was still fighting; I felt spent. Emotionally and mentally worn the heck out. I didn't think any of these guys were the ones for me. And I didn't appreciate the fact that me having a daughter was used in a story line. I just wanted to shut the whole thing down and go home. Obviously no one got a rose on that group date.

The next day I had a one-on-one date with Jef. While I was happy to spend time with him because we hadn't been together in a while, I was still grumpy from what had transpired the night before. Our time together didn't start off well, with a lesson in proper etiquette at some fancy manor where we did more waiting around than learning. Not to mention our teacher was a very matronly and stern-looking woman who didn't attempt to hide the fact that she didn't like me.

Afterward, I remember standing outside a pub and watching Jef playfully poke my naturally beautiful and Bohemian-looking producer with his umbrella. Still feeling the effects of my bad mood, I groaned and thought, *Oh great, now Jef likes her.* I tried my best to squirm out of my cranky pants quickly though. It wasn't serving anyone well. All in all, I enjoyed my time with Jef. While I had never before dated anyone who wore skinny jeans, I appreciated his carefree, fun side. He was easy to talk to and sweet.

I couldn't wait to enjoy dessert that night in the London Eye, a giant observation wheel that cycles these egg-shaped capsules from which you can get a breathtaking 360-degree view of the city. While being in this glass pod looked intimate and romantic on TV, Jef and I weren't the only ones in there. We were surrounded by one of my producers, a soundman and his equipment, and a cameraman and his equipment. While I was used to having the crew around me most of the time, when you're crammed inside such a tiny space, it gets claustrophobic and overwhelming very quickly. There was so much stuff and so many people in there, the windows were fogged up most of the time, blurring what was an exquisite view.

I knew I was going to give Jef a rose that night; I just didn't expect to forget his name in the process (a huge faux pas for a Bachelorette or Bachelor). I was supposed to say, "Jef, will you accept this rose?" which I did, but minus the "Jef" part. My producer immediately looked at me horrified that I would forget the name of a guy who I had not only spent the day with but really liked. I don't know what to say except my mind totally blanked. Maybe it was a warning sign, one out of what would become many. Anyway, I had to do another take, this time making sure I said "Jef."

As I was preparing for the rose ceremony, I realized that I had forgotten to take a certain medication I needed for a facial skin condition. Disturbed by the incident in the pub the night before, I hadn't remembered that morning. Before I started swiping on some mascara, I downed the pill with some bottled water. Ricki was with me as I freshened up. We cuddled on the bed before I had to head down to the lobby to start production when I started feeling tired, out of it. The more I fought the weird feeling, the loopier I got. Ricki was talking to me about castles and dragons, and I remember not having a clue what she was saying but nodding and replying back, "Oh yeah, I bet there were kings and queens in those castles." Good grief!

A few minutes later, while walking into the room where the crew was preparing to film, I felt a solid three sheets to the wind. Suddenly, it hit me. I must have taken the wrong pill. Instead of the skin pill, I probably popped a sleeping pill. (I promise you I'm not a pill popper! I just kept a tiny stash of supplements to help me get some sleep in between the perpetual schedule of events, the different time zones, and the physical demands of the show.)

Knowing I had to start mingling with the bachelors in a bit, I tried to save face and pull myself together. But it's kinda hard when you think you're walking, but you're really stumbling and your eyes can barely stay open. I didn't want to tell anyone what I had accidentally done because I was too embarrassed, but it wasn't like I could hide the fact I was out of it.

By the time I felt like I was floating on air, I realized the pickle I was in. It was bad. Very bad. I stumbled my way in a haze over to someone who looked like one of my producers (thankfully I was right) and grabbed her forcefully by the arm. She could tell something was wrong.

"I think I made a mistake," I whispered a little too loudly, trying hard not to slur.

Her eyes widened and before she could say anything, I reassured her in my half-conscious state, "But don't worry. Everything is going to be fine!" As strung out as I felt, I was cognizant enough to understand an entire crew was depending on me. And there was no way I was going to let them down because of a careless blunder. As production got under way with only a half hour or so before I needed to start filming, I chugged cans and cans of Red Bull, hoping it would counter the sedative effects. And what do you know? It worked.

Aside from sending Alejandro home (you guessed it, we just didn't share a connection), the evening was uneventful—in a good way. I didn't slur my way through the rose ceremony or fall asleep during my announcement to the remaining eight guys that we would be heading off shortly to Dubrovnik, Croatia. I felt great. Perhaps a little too wound up, but that was way better than being dozy.

After my final interview of the evening, actually early morning at this point, I crawled into bed, wrapping my arms tight around my little girl. Though I was barely awake at that point, desperate for some shut-eye, I stared at Ricki's angelic face for a few seconds. Knowing she wasn't able to join me in Croatia, tears fell down my cheeks. I'd have to say good-bye to her in an hour or two so I could leave the hotel by 5:00 a.m. and catch my flight.

Sensing my presence, Ricki started to stir, but her eyes remained shut. My heart broke as I saw the tears flood down her face. "Oh, Ricki," I muttered, hugging her even tighter. As Ricki started full-on sobbing into my chest, all I wanted to do was go home with my little girl. We lay in bed for a while, both bawling our eyes out. When it was almost time for me to leave Ricki, she wiped her tears dry and smiled. As she grinned from wet cheek to wet cheek, I knew that my daughter would be just fine. Me? Not so much.

By the time I headed to the airport, I hadn't slept in more than twenty-four hours, sleeping pill and all. Not to pat myself on the back, but if any Bachelorette ever complains of being tired, I want to be the first to have a little chat with her, to coach her through. If I can wrestle with an Ambien and win, anyone can!

I never would have chosen Croatia as a destination, but when we landed, my eyes fell on one of the most beautiful places I'd ever been. The walled city of Dubrovnik lies at the foot of a mountain surrounded by the clear blue Adriatic Sea. New, bright-orange roof tiles top ancient city walls, as modern joins beautifully with historic. Walking on the cobblestone streets, as Gothic and Renaissance monasteries, palaces, and fountains towered around, was like being transported centuries away. (Fun fact: it's a UNESCO World Heritage Site.)

But the stunning beauty of this European gem couldn't mask the fact that I was miserably homesick. I missed my mom. I missed Ricki. I missed Charlotte. I missed . . . American food. The morning I arrived I asked room service for a bagel, and they had no idea what it was. After explaining it's a round piece of bread with a hole in it, the person on the other line still sounded confused but assured me they would find it somewhere. Heck no! Never mind, I said. I did not want to come off as having a diva moment. I was a Bachelorette for Pete's sake, not the Queen of England.

My first date in Croatia was with Ryan, though the episode made it seem he was my last. I cried beforehand because I didn't want to go. One of my producers laughed when I told her and said, "I'm surprised it took you this long." I sent him home during the date, as well as Travis, who accompanied me on the other one-on-one date.

My feelings for Arie started getting shaky at this point. During the course of filming, I discovered that one of the producers had dated him years ago. She apologized for not sharing with me, but I was really upset at Arie for keeping the information mum.

Aric and I had a one-on-one date in Prague. With my tour book in hand and a carefully planned itinerary from the producers, he and I strolled around the crowded streets of old Europe as street artists and musicians showed off their talents to passing tourists and locals. By the time we reached the stunning medieval Charles Bridge that connects two parts of the city and is dotted with replicas of seventeenth-century statues, I tried to draw the information out of Arie with the skills of a very inept Spanish Inquisitor. As we rubbed the sculpture of Saint John of Nepomuk on the bridge, which, legend has it, is supposed to bring good fortune, I was getting more and more angry.

Eventually, Arie and I talked, but things changed from that point on between us. Oh, I was attracted to him. I enjoyed his company. I liked kissing him. And there was no denying we had an intense connection, but this whole situation dampened my feelings.

By this point, Jef was attracting my attention more. Unfortunately, sometimes not for the best reasons, though I couldn't see it at the time. While we were in Prague, I had heard that Jef had jumped off the balcony in his hotel room and onto another and almost got kicked out by the manager as a result. He was asked to apologize to the hotel guest whose balcony he landed on, and though he did, Jef laughed about the situation. To him, it was a joke. A prank.

I'm sad to report that I thought his behavior reflected his edge—his fun, spontaneous, and crazy side. It didn't occur to me that these were red flags of immaturity. Instead of letting this information sink in for what it was worth, I allowed my naivety to rule over good old common sense.

In past relationships, I often ignored what were obvious

warning signs. I viewed disrespectful behavior as a challenge, often being drawn to bad boys and hoping I could tame them and turn them into normal-relationship material. One guy I dated briefly went for days without calling on several occasions. I assumed he was playing hard to get. I liked that. But really, he was just being a jerk. Another guy I dated left me stranded on our date, saying later that he "wasn't a taxi service." I knew he'd had a painful past, so I chose to believe the only reason he was hurting me was because he was hurt, and if I continued to be my sweet, reassuring, and understanding self, I could change him for the better.

Apparently, I carried some of these awfully misguided notions on the show. While I had changed and grown emotionally in many aspects, I still wasn't the smartest when it came to relationships, namely picking a guy who would be a good fit for my life and Ricki's (one of the reasons I'd been single for so long). With that said, at the time, I had a ton of fun with Jef on our one-on-one.

Hometown dates were next. There was no doubt in my mind I was going to pick Jef for one. I also chose Arie even though I wasn't totally over his silence about dating my producer. And then Sean was a shoo-in. Having said good-bye to Doug earlier in Croatia, it was a toss-up between John, who was from Missouri, or Chicago-hailing Chris. I opted to take a chance in the Windy City.

eleven

Though it was a long week of meeting all the families, the experience was sweet. I was honored to be introduced into the guys' worlds, getting to know their parents and siblings, who beamed with pride and joy.

Chris showed me around Chicago and took me to lunch in a Polish restaurant, celebrating his heritage. Then we spent time with his parents and two sisters. Later that day Chris's dad pulled me aside and asked if he was correct in assuming he "sensed some love" between his son and me. I nodded and said yes. At the time my emotions were a swirling mess, so it was hard to logically process exactly what I was feeling.

Utah was breathtaking, and Jef's siblings and their kids were super sweet. His parents were away on a missions trip and unfortunately couldn't make it. Jef and I had a blast skeet shooting, and I was very impressed that this guy in skinny jeans was an awesome shot. At the end of our date, he read me a letter that he wrote to me on the plane. He spoke of how our relationship was meant to be and that he was completely in love with me. What impressed me most was his expression of love for Ricki and how he promised to always be there for her.

His words touched me, and I was so grateful for his openness and honesty.

I met up with Arie in Scottsdale, Arizona. Before I met his parents, he told me, in a warning-like fashion, "They're European. They're different, Emily. They say what's on their minds." I didn't mind. I mean, I was nervous, as any normal girl would be meeting the parents of someone she liked. But nothing prepared me for the awkwardness that would ensue. While his parents and brothers were warm and welcoming at first, there was a long period of our conversation where his parents broke off in Dutch for a while. I just sat there, not understanding a word they said, but wondering what on earth they were talking about. It made me feel quite uncomfortable.

Being with Sean and his family in Dallas was a representation of everything I wanted to be, an ideal image of the perfect boyfriend and his perfect family. And yes, when he pulled the "I live at home with my parents" joke, I admit, I was really nervous for a second. And quite relieved that he did not, in fact, live at home with a room full of stuffed animals. Sean's family was sweet, inviting. And I had a great time with all of them.

By the time I ended up in Los Angeles for the rose ceremony, I was exhausted. But I was also torn about having to say goodbye to someone. Getting sent home right after the hometown dates stunk probably as bad as getting eliminated during the first rose ceremony. You can't help but wonder if it's because your family was perceived as nuts, which, in Chris's case, was definitely not true. Though I enjoyed spending time with him, I didn't feel our connection had grown significantly, at least not enough to continue to pursue the relationship. (Gosh, it's so odd to even use the word *relationship* when you're dealing with multiple guys, but there's no other way to say it.)

As I was getting ready for bed before Jef, Arie, Sean, and I would head off to Curacao the next day, I heard a knock on my door. It was Jef. It was nice to hang out with him without cameras, mics, and other equipment around. That night he gave me a turquoise ring he had bought for me during our stay in Croatia. Our time together wasn't long, but it definitely affirmed my feelings for him.

Ricki was with me when my love pilgrimage advanced to the colorful and historic Dutch island of Curacao. We hunkered down in a secluded and gorgeous house that overlooked glimmering indigo waters. When I wasn't filming, Ricki and I played and swam in the pool and on the beach. Spending time with her gave me some relief from the anxiety I struggled with trying to figure out whether Sean, Arie, or Jef was the best match for our future.

All the one-on-one dates were fun, but my date with Arie was particularly memorable. He and I went swimming with dolphins in the ocean. Which is super cool, right? I mean, who doesn't love dolphins? They're adorable, squeaky, and cuddly! But not being the best swimmer and treading water—sans a life jacket—that's twenty or thirty feet deep while sizable waves break right over you kinda pulls the plug on the whole cute-dolphin thing. I'd swum with these lovable creatures before, but in a pool. Where you can stand. And touch the ground. And if you start to feel apprehensive, you can make a fast break out of the water.

While my attitude was far from pleasant, Arie made the best of it, something I really appreciated about him. He just laughed and held on to me protectively as waves surged and dolphins squealed.

Arie asked me a lot of questions about my faith. He knew I wanted to go on a missions trip to Africa one day, and we got into a conversation about God.

"Where does your faith in God come from?" he asked.

It was a loaded question but one I could answer easily. "From having nothing else," I told him. "After the accident, I had nothing. No one understood what I was going through and I felt all alone. Having a relationship with God gave me a hope for my future."

Arie nodded thoughtfully. I appreciated his deep questions. He was willing to go beneath the surface with me, something that made our conversations run deeper than the run-of-the-mill Bachelorette "How-are-you-I'm-having-fun-and-I-like-you-a-lot" conversations.

I had fun with all three guys. I enjoyed their company. They were all really nice guys with great qualities. Whenever I spent time with each of them alone, in that moment, I felt connected to whomever I was with. It was hard not to, being in romantic settings, frolicking on white beaches, jumping off sailboats into crystal seas, having sunset picnics on the beach, enjoying delicious candlelight dinners. I'd be a robot if my feelings didn't gush on these amazing dates. It was easy to block out the other guys and focus on whomever I was with at the moment—not a particularly good sign when you're thinking about marriage. I had to say good-bye to one of them. I prayed wholeheartedly that I'd make the right decision.

My heart was weighed down not only by having to let one of the guys go but also because I wondered about the authenticity of my relationships with them, despite being so close to the finish line. I didn't know if the guys liked me— Emily Maynard—or if they were falling in love with Emily the Bachelorette. Were their feelings sincere? Did they simply want to win? Was it a mixture of both?

As the first rose ceremony in Curacao drew near, the more I knew I felt closer to Jef and Arie than I did to Sean. Sean was a great guy, stunningly good looking and sweet. I liked him as a person and, for sure, we had formed a friendship. But I felt more comfortable with the other two. Conversations with Jef and Arie flowed pretty easily. With Sean, I noticed a lot more awkward silence where producers would have to interrupt our time and chime in with suggestions for topics of discussion.

Sean also didn't ask a ton of questions about me or my life, so I didn't feel our relationship had entered anywhere beyond a surface level. But I'll admit, being with him made me want to live the life of a perfect wife and have the perfect family, and many times I told him I was excited to possibly share a future with him. Looking back, I feel I probably led him on. Still, saying good-bye to Sean broke my heart. I'll never forget sitting with him on the bench outside the villa, mostly in silence. Sean didn't know what to say. I didn't know what to say. I tried to explain my feelings to him, but at this point there were no words I could offer to justify letting him go, at least not in his eyes.

"I'm not sure what to say," Sean began.

I didn't know either. "What are you thinking about?" I asked.

"I feel kinda stupid," he confessed. That broke my heart. That was the last thing I wanted him to feel. We talked for a bit after that, a lot of tears peppering my apologies. It was a hard moment for many reasons.

After I walked Sean to the waiting car, I returned to that same bench and sobbed. Sadness aside, I knew he would move on and have his pick of wonderful and beautiful women. I also knew one day he would make a great Bachelor. I was right. Sean got engaged to Catherine Giudici on the season 17 finale, and ten months later the two of them wed in *The Bachelor*'s first live TV wedding. I wish the two of them all the best!

My parents, my brother, Ernie, and his girlfriend flew down for a few days to meet and spend time with Jef and Arie. I was delighted to have my parents be a part of the show. They were proud of me, that I was taking a chance, however extreme, at finding love. Their friends were blasting them with so many questions about this journey, and I knew being able to share the final moments of the show on camera with me would give them some giggles and some well-deserved bragging rights to their friends.

Mom, Dad, and Ernie were open hearted and gracious toward the two remaining guys. While I was grateful to have my family's support at such a critical time in my life, they weren't much help. They liked both Jef and Arie, and if they had an opinion of whom they would choose for me, they didn't say. I did have a feeling my dad was rooting for Arie because he was more of a man's man than Jef. Dad didn't understand the whole skinny-jeans-and-Chucks ensemble.

The only specific my mother told me was, "Don't get engaged." Which, to me, was a no-brainer. While the producers had known from the start that I didn't want to walk away from the show with a fiancé, but only with a serious boyfriend, that week I made sure to remind them. I didn't want any sur-prises. I wasn't ready for that kind of commitment, and I didn't want to repeat the same mistake I made with Brad.

When I had the Last Chance Date with Jef, I knew I would pick him. I loved the walk we had on the beach where we talked about our future, about family. I felt so strongly about him, I brought him to meet Ricki, who was playing in the pool, introducing him as my friend. The three of us had a great time together, and I really thought Jef and I had a chance, that a relationship could work. That being said, Jef knew I didn't want to get engaged on the show, which put me at ease that our relationship wouldn't progress any further than I was willing to go.

But before Jef and I could take our steps forward, I had to say good-bye to Arie. I didn't have the heart to go through with our Last Chance Date. It didn't seem fair. I didn't have a clue what I was going to say. How do you initiate a conversation that would end with a forever good-bye? As I walked toward Arie that day, I hoped he could read my mind, that he could see at least from the expression on my face that something was amiss. I wished with all my heart that even before I had the chance to stutter my way through our farewell, he would knowingly just walk away, without even having to say anything. But that didn't happen. When Arie saw me, he started rubbing on my arm the love potion he had made with one of the locals.

We spent a while together, much longer than what you see on TV. And the experience was much more emotional. While Arie sat stunned, I cried, "I don't know what to say," sobs choking my voice. I wasn't the only one with tears in my eyes. Many of the crew members who surrounded us were crying as well.

"Don't say anything," he replied and started walking away.

My heart fell as I walked after Arie, not wanting to end the moment that way.

"I don't know what you want, Emily. Thank you for sparing me the embarrassment tomorrow. I appreciate that," he said after he gave me a hug, and we walked to the waiting car.

It broke my heart to have to end the relationship with Arie, but I had to make a decision. I had to send someone home. It wasn't that I didn't like him or that I wasn't attracted to him or that the time we spent together was a sham. I couldn't continue getting to know two men; I had to choose one.

And then, there was just one.

I was a hopeful bundle of nerves during the final rose ceremony, waiting for Jef on a platform rising above a cobblestone street and surrounded by gorgeous white, purple, and fuchsia tropical flowers. The first thing I noticed when Jef arrived was his pants. They were tight. Before anything dirty crosses your mind, hear me out. I felt relieved because there was no way a boxed ring would fit in those tight pants. *Phew!* I thought to myself. I had dodged a bullet!

When Ashley H. was on *The Bachelorette*, I remember watching the final rose ceremony when she was about to say good-bye to Ben Flajnik. It was gut wrenching to watch him get down on one knee and propose to her before she got those words out. I didn't want that to happen between Jef and me. So in order to avoid a potentially devastating moment on camera, I had planned to be watchful, to pay attention to his every move so in case he started dropping down into proposal position, I could stop him immediately.

When I saw what was clearly the absence of a ring, my guard came tumbling down. And rather than be suspect of any sudden movement, I could appreciate the moment. Big mistake. Jef started sharing his feelings, telling me things that sounded very much like the spiel you hear right before a proposal. He said, "What I'm about to ask you is a forever thing," and my mind froze.

I liked Jef. I was even pretty sure I was falling in love with him, but getting married to him wasn't the next thing I wanted to do in my life. I wanted to pursue a deeper relationship off camera before we made any huge decisions. But before I knew it, he was down on one knee asking me to marry him. I couldn't even begin to process what was happening, and I couldn't for the life of me stop the inevitable.

I waited for a long time before I said yes. Well, when you're silent for a minute or two after an important question, that's considered a long time. I sped my way through a hundred questions as I stared at Jef in silence. *What am I going to do? How would he react if I said no? What would the producers think? What would people think? Would everyone hate me?*

I felt an enormous burden of pressure as the cameramen steadied their cameras at us, waiting, as Jef continued to look deep into my eyes, waiting. And despite everything in me that screamed a hundred shades of no, despite my reservation, despite my adamant request that I didn't want to get engaged, one that could not have been made any clearer to the producers, I gulped inwardly and said, "Yes."

The scene after uttering that one word was exactly the

same as when I said it to Brad. Equipment was shut down, turned off, unplugged, wrapped up, and the crew started making their way off the island. Well, wait a minute. They did film Ricki running toward us after the proposal (though she was unaware of what exactly had just gone down).

I'm almost embarrassed to say this, but the second I saw my sweet daughter, her long ponytail flapping in the wind, I knew I shouldn't have gotten engaged. I wondered how a relationship with Jef was going to work, how he would fit into Ricki's life, if he was, in fact, ready to be a stepparent. The fears flooded through me, making me question every bit of hope I had that things between Jef and me stood, at least, a chance. Though my thoughts swirled in overwhelming circles, I smiled and at least on the outside looked happy.

The three of us didn't spend much time together after that rendezvous. Jef left to pack up his stuff and was going to meet me later that night at a house where we'd stay for the next three or four days. Ricki and I went back to my house on the island, hugging, playing, and snuggling before she headed back to Charlotte.

Unlike after my first TV proposal, Jef and I had so much fun when the cameras were off. I loved his carefree, playful vibe; it made it easy for me to be just as silly. I wasn't bored any minute of the time we spent together. One time Jef stole a pair of surfboards from this random dock, assuring me with a wink in his eye not to worry because, "It's not like we're going to keep them. We're going to return them after we're done using them." The better part of my nature thought it was rude and disrespectful, but another part of me, the former Emily who had a thing for bad boys, thought it was amusing. After our escapade of finally being alone, Jef returned to Utah and I to Charlotte.

A day or two after returning to North Carolina, a slight sense of normalcy resumed. I was home. No cameras. No producers. Though, as they had become incredible friends, I missed being around my producers. I was washing the dishes the first night back and simultaneously yelling at Ricki and her friend, engrossed in dressing up Barbies, to get moving because we had to leave soon for soccer or something or other.

"Let's go, Ricki!" I called out again, this time a bit more forcefully, just when I heard the doorbell ring. Looking through the glass front door, I saw a young woman standing outside. I assumed she was a *Bachelorette* fan and hurriedly said through the pane, "Hi, can I help you?" feeling a little more peeved because time was ticking without mercy and this distraction was delaying the day's events even more.

"Hi," the woman said politely. She looked uneasy, and not in a good or cute way, which set me a bit on edge. "My name is Christina. I'm Arie's friend."

"Hi," I replied, still feeling rushed and now a little paranoid. Arie's friend? I didn't trust that. Seemed too peculiar. I wondered if she was really a journalist or maybe even paparazzi. Though she seemed harmless and didn't necessarily give off a bad vibe, my suspicions stayed strong.

"Arie's here," she blurted out.

"Okay, cool," I said, my poker face intact. I started to get real worried she was trying to squeeze information out of me to spoil the show. I don't know what I was thinking, but I invited her in. Dumb, right? At this point, I was so late and all I could think about was getting out of the house as quickly as possible. So if talking to her for a minute would help do that, so be it. I figured she could do the talking while I continued to get ready to leave.

As I finished rinsing the dishes, Christina spoke. "I know you didn't pick Arie."

I didn't say a word and fought to maintain an expressionless face. In my heart, I didn't know what to believe. I just stood there, suds dripping from the yellow gloves.

"Arie's here," she continued. "He's in a car right around the corner and wants to talk to you. He's not ready to give up on you. He loves you. And he knows the two of you are meant to be."

Well, I just about died inside, still standing in silence, while Christina whipped out her phone, dialed a number, and handed it to me. When I put the receiver up to my ear and heard the "Hey Emily" on the other line, my heart dropped. It was Arie. It really was him.

"I'm around the corner," he said. "Sitting in a park parking lot. I need to see you."

I won't lie. A part of me wanted to see him. But I also wanted to respect Jef. After all, he was the one I had chosen, and I had to honor that decision. This was too big of a deal to even think about being wishy-washy. I had to put what I wanted aside because I knew how much me seeing Arie would upset Jef. Even if I justified spending a few minutes with the guy just as a friend, I knew deep down it wasn't a good idea.

"I'll call you later," I told Arie. "After Ricki goes to sleep."

I was shaken up when Christina finally left. I didn't expect Arie to reach out so boldly, to fly into my hometown, for Pete's sake, in what seemed like an effort to win me back. It threw me off, especially the fact that I did want to see him. When Ricki, her friend, and I eventually left the house, my phone buzzed with calls and texts from Arie and Christina. I never answered or replied to any of their messages.

I was scared. Scared because being in contact with Arie would jeopardize my contract with ABC, and there was no way I wanted to be sued by a media giant. I was scared that paparazzi would somehow snap a picture of Arie by my house, or heaven forbid, us together. I was scared because what if I saw him and all these feelings started rushing back? I wanted to try to make things work with Jef, and I didn't want to plant any seeds of distrust, especially so early on. I never called Arie back. Later, I did tell Jef what had happened and his response was as expected—ticked off.

Around ten that night, as I was getting ready for bed, the doorbell rang. My heart raced as I splashed water on my face to wash off the remnants of the day's makeup. I had a feeling it might be Arie. While I didn't answer the door or even go downstairs right away, I snuck a peek outside my window. As dark as it was, sure enough, I could make out his face as he drove off into the night.

My hands shook as I headed down the stairs and opened the front door, peering to the left and right to make sure no paparazzi was anywhere near. As I looked down, I noticed a sealed FedEx envelope. I quickly scooped up the package and ran back into the house, just as I heard a text message notification blaring from my phone. It was Arie.

I left you my journal so you can read through it and
see how I feel about you.

I didn't open the envelope, but I knew what he was talking about. Weeks earlier, I had given Arie, off camera, a journal from Dollywood. I remembered that day well. As I was getting to know him, I could see he was on a soul search. And being on the show, as hard as it could be at times, was a great opportunity to learn about yourself, to dig deep and explore, maybe even figure out, some of the empty, wandering, or broken parts. I had encouraged Arie to do this, hoping a journal would be a great prompt.

I won't lie. I wanted to tear open the package and flip through those pages. But I knew doing so would only trigger memories and emotions that I wasn't prepared to deal with. Just because I let Arie go didn't mean I automatically shut down my feelings for him. They were still there. Not as strong as the ones I had for Jef, but nonetheless, still there. I left the package on the kitchen table, sealed.

It was either late that same night or the next day that I called one of my producers and told her Arie had shown up at my house and had left a journal. I had to tell the producers the truth, even though I was worried it might get Arie in trouble. If anything had leaked to the press about the incident, I would have been in far worse trouble. Later, I mailed the package back to the network producers.

I remained hopeful about my relationship with Jef, but as weeks and months passed, it was obvious our love life off camera was a far cry from what I had envisioned. Turns out, we were different people who wanted different things. The pictures we painted of our futures didn't align and definitely didn't mesh. And this is how I found myself crying in the New York hotel room, my producer by my side, while on a tour of media appearances (reread the prologue to refresh your memory) as the new Bachelorette who finally found love again. Except, of course, I really hadn't. I will say what I appreciated about Jef was his support when the media firestorm blew up in the summer of 2012.

More headlines, mostly negative ones, tore me apart, calling me a "bad person," accusing me of having had all these "dark secrets," describing me as a diva, mean, and giving lists of reasons why the relationship between Jef and me wouldn't work out, which seemed to always have to do with . . . me. Oh yeah, and then there were the accusations that I demanded the most expensive and designer duds for my wardrobe. For the record, I had nothing to do with choosing what I was going to wear. That was all on the network stylists. Oh, I loved what they picked out, of course, but that was totally their own doing.

I can't tell you how many times right before I went online to read these awful articles that I felt the nudge of the Holy Spirit urging me not to do it. *Close the window. Turn the computer off. Read My Word instead.* And each time, aware of the prompting, I ignored it and did my own thing. Which was really dumb because every single time I'd log off, I always felt worse, many times sick to my stomach.

While I didn't lean much on my last relationship for support as my reputation and character were being torn to bits, Jef did help me through some tough times, reminding me the printed words were just lies and par for the course. He encouraged me not to take the attention so seriously. "Just laugh about it," he offered. I appreciated the great advice, but it wasn't easy to follow through. And I quickly spiraled downward into a depression.

At one point, just like last time, I switched on reclusive mode. I stayed at home a lot, taking Ricki to school and her activities, of course, but that was about it. When I get stressed, my OCD kicks in, and I turn into a cleaning and organizing maniac. So while the tabloids blared ungenerous headlines, I went through every drawer in every piece of furniture in every room of my house, throwing out the junk and meticulously organizing everything by color or size. We're talking pens, Sharpies, batteries, clothing, socks, pots, pans, utensils, you name it. I even took the liberty of collecting all the magazines I had purchased that featured articles about the show or me (don't judge me, I was a glutton for punishment back then) and organized them chronologically by month and year in plastic bins identified by printed labels.

I also mopped every corner of the house, dusted every baseboard in every room, and vacuumed every inch of carpet, taking painstaking care to spot-clean muddy footprints and spilled juice as well. Bananas, I get it. Maybe I could have transferred that energy into doing something productive for society, but even thinking of going anywhere gave me suffocating anxiety. I will say my obsession indulgence did help keep some of the nervous energy at bay.

Though my house was spotless, my relationship with Jef was deteriorating. We were together for a couple of months. He even moved to Charlotte at one point, in hopes that being geographically close would relieve some of the pressure that was building in our relationship. Not so much. I was trying so hard to make things work between Jef and me that my emotional well-being took quite a beating. I felt battered. I looked exhausted. I could barely smile. The only person I felt I could talk to was my mom, but I didn't. I knew what she would say—that I shouldn't have said yes.

At one point, Jef and I saw a Mormon marriage counselor, hoping someone with experience could help resolve some of our differences. But it didn't help. And we were only a fight away from breaking up for good. I'll never forget sitting on my kitchen table after the last argument we had. He stormed out of the house and though I was tempted to chase after him, I remember the Holy Spirit speaking to my heart as clear as day. *Let him go.*

And I did.

I can't even begin to tell you how devastated I felt saying good-bye to yet another failed relationship, and a televised one at that. It was heartbreaking, embarrassing, and I was utterly broken, too exhausted to pick up the pieces this time around. I isolated myself from others, the world, as much as possible after the breakup. When I wasn't with Ricki, I spent my time curled up on my bed in a fetal position, crying. It took about a month or two for stories about our wrecked love life to die down and for the paparazzi that had been camped out in this quiet North Carolina town to turn their attention toward another reality TV hot mess.

While I started settling back into life as a regular soccer mom, I was being challenged in my spiritual life. I was ashamed, even regretful, of some of the choices I had made on and off the show. Battling confusion, I wondered about the peace I was so confident I had felt when I opted to be on *The*

Bachelorette. I didn't make it up. It was real. I know it was. I felt it so strongly in my heart. But how real could it have been given the outcome? Given the failed relationships? Given the media lashings? Had God really led me to do the show as I had truly believed He had? I began to wonder how I could even trust that whenever I prayed, I was talking to God. What if I was talking to myself? Or the devil? Or absolutely nothing?

All my doubts, questioning, and confusion aside, I felt God trying to shake me out of my emotional, but more so spiritual, slump. It wasn't an audible voice that I heard, but in my heart, and with each passing day I could hear His words echoing in my heart. *You say you've given your life to Me, but you keep doing the same foolish things over and over. Choosing the wrong relationships, turning men and even the opinions of others into idols. Enough already. You need to give Me your heart.*

I thought I had. I really did. But I was learning, ever so slowly, that there's a big difference between saying a few prayers and calling yourself a Christian and really committing to the faith life, with words, actions, deeds—you know, the whole nine yards. I read or heard Francis Chan ask, "Has your relationship with God changed the way you live your life?"* The question provoked me, forcing me to really think about what it meant to surrender your heart to God. Was it a one-time deal? Saying a carefully constructed prayer you learn in church? Going to church? What did a faith commitment look like? What did I have to give up? What did I have to do more of? Or less of? How did I know my words, my actions, my thoughts were as sincere as I imagined?

---

* Francis Chan, *Crazy Love* (Colorado Springs: David C. Cook, 2013), 67.

As the questions came with fury, I could feel God working in me, changing me, shifting my perspective, opening wide my spiritual eyes for the first time. I was stretching, growing, and beginning to loosen my grip from what really were, in fact, idols.

I was finally letting God do His job. And He was allowing me to start over.

twelve

'll never forget the last time I browsed through the tabloids online. Clicking through a few websites, feeling more
depressed the longer I lingered on a particular article or blog,
I felt the Holy Spirit prompt me in a forceful yet gentle way.

Open your Bible.

This time, I listened.

I closed my computer and grabbed my Bible off a nearby
counter. I didn't know if I was supposed to look for something
specific or what. Staring at the leather-bound book, I didn't
know where to start. So I flipped over to the concordance and
looked up the word *judgment*. I was so tormented by the negative print about me and my relationship with Jef, I wanted to
know what the Bible had to say about judging others. I don't
remember what exactly I read, but that simple act of obedience, that detour from what had turned into a terrible habit of
reading discouraging trash daily, changed my life. And through
that one simple act of obedience, I finally said yes. But this
time, to God.

I started reading the Bible regularly that day. Not books
about the Bible, not devotions quoting Bible passages, not

blogs about the Bible—but the actual Word of God. I pored over Scripture, soaking in stories of flawed people who God still used even though they had missed the mark, many of them more than once. And for the first time in my life, I felt I was getting to know the heart of God. I was beginning to see more clearly who He was and what His character was like. Never before had I felt so close to God. I began to realize that the lack of relationship wasn't because He wasn't willing or able or wanting to draw closer to me; the issue was mine. I didn't draw near. I didn't take a step toward Him. I didn't pay attention to Him, His voice, His nudges.

But things were different now. In making a commitment to wholeheartedly follow God, I began to discover who I was in Christ, gaining a newfound confidence in His grace, His mercy, His love.

The more time I spent with God, praying and reading His Word, I realized there were a lot of things I had to ask forgiveness for. I had made some poor choices that had painful results. From a purity standpoint, I wish I hadn't given away my sexuality. I wish I would have waited until I got married and given that gift to my husband, no matter how long that took. With all my relationships, having sex before marriage had seemed so easy to justify.

I'm young.

I'm in love.

God knows my heart.

He knows I'm not a bad person.

I mean, it's not like I'm doing drugs or committing murder.

But there were so many repercussions to not respecting that part of my being and not honoring God in my choices. Having sex before marriage created unhealthy emotional attachments. It put me at risk for diseases. It dishonored God. And though Ricki is one of the best things that has ever happened to me, being a single mother so young is the hardest thing I've ever had to do in my life.

Regardless of my mistakes, I rested in faith, knowing that through God's grace, because Jesus had willfully chosen to give up His life for me on the cross, and no matter how undeserving I felt—and I did—I was forgiven. I was loved. And I was redeemed. Wow! Just writing these words fires me up and amazes me at how God has so powerfully changed my life.

The more I fell in love with Jesus, the more I changed. The more I grew. I didn't want to be known as that girl from that dating show; I wanted to be known for being a woman who reflects Christ's love, who freely gives His grace to others, whose faith is marked by actions and words.

As I was being transformed bit by bit, I still struggled at times with anxiety, fearful of what I would hear in the media about my breakup with Jef or other tales and gossip. I found the more I dug into the Bible, the more relief I felt from reading the words of God. The ancient text of Esther was one biblical story that really moved me to believe that God is bigger than any problem or emotion I face. This sacred narrative introduces us to Esther, a beautiful and young Hebrew woman. Without a say in the matter, she was chosen to be the queen of a Persian king. Smitten by her, the king was also ignorant of her ethnicity.

Through her cousin Mordecai, Esther learned of a plot drummed up by the king's prime minister to have the Jews massacred. Mordecai pleaded with Esther to beg the king for mercy. Understandably, this young woman was not quite gung ho about approaching the king unsummoned, something that would likely get her killed. But Esther's cousin was persistent and told her God was with her, that He'd always been. And then Mordecai challenged Esther by reminding her of the obvious—that she was a Jewish woman who found herself as a queen in the royal palace. "You're here for such a time as this," Mordecai pointed out.

For such a time as this. Could it be that Esther was in such a position to help save her people from death? Really?

I won't retell every detail of the story (I encourage you to read the text on your own), but Esther did talk to the king, with knees shaking and palms sweating, I imagine. And the king did grant her favor and extinguish the murderous plot, also promoting Mordecai in the process. Reading this story brought me a hope I never had. I couldn't get the words *for such a time as this* out of my head, especially because looking back at what I considered failed experiences at being on the reality shows, I wondered if there was an underlying reason why they even happened.

I was also moved by what I read in Jeremiah 29:11: "'For I know the plans I have for you,' declares the LORD, 'plans to prosper you and not to harm you, plans to give you hope and a future'" (NIV). I wondered if God could use my experiences to help grow His kingdom somehow, maybe even redeem my mistakes and misguided steps to help a young girl switch directions in her own life, to avoid some of the things I went through. But that wasn't for me to decide or figure out. All I needed to do was stay in the moment, live my life, continue to be a good mom, and most important, love and be obedient to my Savior.

In January 2013, I was in Los Angeles when I got a text from Tyler. He asked if I would tweet about an upcoming Justice Conference, a gathering of leaders, visionaries, and students from different faiths to talk about and promote social justice issues. I agreed on one condition.

You have to take me to dinner.

Tyler accepted my proposal, saying something like he must be a glutton for punishment.

We had our first date a week or so later, on the day of the worst winter storm of the year. A few inches of snow accumulated before freezing rain fell over our city, blanketing the ground in dangerous sheets of ice. While this may be the norm for the northern part of the country, North Carolina doesn't experience many severe winter storms, and so our area was ill prepared (understatement). Schools were closed. Power lines were down. Accidents abounded on the slippery roadways. Many of the local residences and businesses were without electricity. It was mayhem.

I am embarrassed to admit this, but the weather was so bad, I wanted to cancel. As smoking hot as Tyler was, all I wanted to do was get in my pajamas and curl up in bed under warm blankets. There was no way I wanted to go out in such bleary and cold weather. Yet, I didn't want Tyler thinking I was a flake. Also, our mutual friend Lori had recently been pestering me to go out with Tyler. She was a smart gal, not one to blow smoke, so I trusted her.

Despite the storm, neither one of us bailed—and thank goodness for that. Tyler and I settled on meeting at a nice, but as it turned out very stuffy, restaurant in town. It was one of the few places that was open. Except for a cook, a waitress, and a hostess, the place was empty. Dinner was delish, but so quiet that it was weird to have a conversation with almost everyone within earshot. After Tyler picked up the tab, we decided to have dessert at a nearby lounge, Zinc, which had a surprisingly large crowd in spite of the icy conditions outside.

As we indulged in mouthwatering chocolate delicacies, I was so glad I hadn't canceled the date. Tyler and I talked for hours. We talked about our faith, our pasts, our families, our futures, what we were looking for in life, in love. He was very mature and responsible, and he had his life together and figured out. What attracted me to Tyler the most was his deep faith. He didn't just call himself a Christian or simply believe in God; his spiritual life was personal, deep, and real. I really liked that. And I really liked him.

While a part of me was used to guys blowing up my phone with voicemails and text messages, Tyler took his time communicating with me, waiting a day or two to call and ask me out again. He didn't play games, but he wasn't desperate. It was a balance I wasn't quite used to. Maybe this is sad to say, but Tyler was the first guy I liked in a long time who didn't have a jerk edge or whom I wasn't trying to fix or turn into someone else. Tyler was Tyler, and I had no desire, and no need, to change him. As a matter of fact, he was beginning to inspire me with his passion for Jesus and his confidence in following God's plan, not his own, for his life.

Tyler and I continued to see each other regularly, and he quickly became my best friend. Our relationship was very different from the others. He got me on every level, knowing when to give me space when I was in a bratty mood, unlike other guys who would pick fights with me instead of leave me well enough alone. Tyler was the most confident guy I had ever met, and even though he has reasons upon reasons to be self-assured, his confidence comes only from God and his identity in Christ.

Tyler was also the most positive male figure in Ricki's life. When we dated, he would come over with his yellow lab, Knox, and play with Ricki, who was as much of an animal lover as myself. She always had a blast with Tyler, who has a knack for making anyone feel comfortable. And while she was immediately enamored by Knox and his playful ways, I noticed she was beginning to dig Tyler just as much.

But the closer Tyler and I got, the more I worried about how Ricki would feel about him, knowing he was my serious boyfriend and possibly, down the road, more. My daughter has always been very protective of me, and I have never wanted her to feel second place to anyone, especially not a man. Knowing my fears, Tyler prayed about it, asking God to soften Ricki's heart and for opportunities for them to build a relationship. And you know what? God answered our prayers.

Tyler and Ricki developed a sweet and strong friendship organically, without my needing to intervene, manipulate conversations to ensure they were talking, or even desperately try to convince Ricki of what an amazing guy he was. They didn't need my help. As a matter of fact, Ricki and Tyler started calling me the "fun police," pouting if I tried to finagle my way into one of their fun activities, like doing cartwheels or playing Frisbee with Knox. I couldn't help but feel that Tyler was a gift from God to Ricki. While I never used the word *boyfriend* when talking about him with Ricki, she was no dummy. Tyler was around enough for her to do the math and figure out we were a couple.

Though we had talked about getting married and our relationship was headed in that direction, Tyler and I didn't discuss details, like dates and the like. But considering our relationship was serious, we chose to attend a premarital class in church. Before each session, we would both pray, separately, that God would open our eyes to anything that would hinder our relationship from taking the next step. If there was a reason we shouldn't be together or if it wasn't a part of God's plan for our lives, we wanted to be the first ones to know. Counseling was rough. We had some uncomfortable but necessary conversations about life, finances, goals, even our theological differences. But never did I feel that we were doing something wrong. There weren't any red flags that our relationship would end up as a total disaster. As 2013 drew to a close, I wrote in my journal about my feelings for Tyler.

> I'm scared of telling the world about my relationship with Tyler, only for it to end in another disaster. I know it's asking a lot and to be honest, I feel like God You have given me some indication of what You want for my life, but please give me signs in my heart that Tyler is the one for me, the one you have designed for me to marry. I don't want to confuse my wants for Yours anymore. Lord, I'm truly so thankful for all the changes in my life, my newfound happiness and confidence.

A year from our first date, Tyler asked me to marry him. Ricki, he, and I had come back from a short vacation over the holidays. Before we left, I had a feeling he would propose on the trip, specifically on New Year's. You know, the start of a new year, the start of a new level of relationship. Blah, blah, blah. But I was wrong. And, as much as I tried to hide it, a bit disappointed.

The morning after our trip, Tyler surprised Ricki and me by coming over early in the morning and setting up the kitchen for a mouthwatering breakfast. But there was more than orange juice, waffle mix, and a beautifully set table in the kitchen. The room was also filled with colorful, fresh-cut flowers in every corner and lanterns with glowing tea lights on the counters. Best of all, there was a scrapbook that Tyler had made for Ricki and me, complete with ticket stubs and other memorabilia from our dates and fun times together. I just about came undone with joy. This was just the sweetest thing Tyler had ever done.

Before we dove into breakfast, Tyler sat Ricki and me down and opened up his Bible. He began reading us some of his favorite verses and then pulled out his journal, reminiscing about our journey and the important and memorable steps along the way. It still didn't dawn on me that this was it, the big moment, until he pulled out a small gold ring and gave it to Ricki, saying, "With your permission, I'd like to ask your mom to be my wife." My little girl shrieked an ear-shattering "Yes!" as my jaw dropped. And then, Tyler got down on one knee.

"Emily Maynard, will you marry me?" And with that question, he held out a box of stunning bands. Earlier, I had mentioned to Tyler that I didn't want a traditional engagement ring. While I was on *The Bachelor*, I noticed one of the producers wore a collection of beautiful bands on her left ring finger. She told me each ring was from the different places she and her husband had traveled to and had significant meaning. I loved that idea and had shared it with Tyler. While he honored my desire, my soon-to-be fiancé went over and beyond, including some bling in the collection of rings. The rings couldn't have been more "me." Obviously, I accepted the proposal wholeheartedly.

Tyler and I got married on June 7, 2014, with Ricki by my side as my maid of honor. And with the help of an amazing wedding planner, Ivy Robinson, the day was perfect. Not only did she create a breathtaking outdoor extravaganza with the perfect mix of elegant and rustic, colored in delicate hues of blush and gold—she did it all in just under three months! Stylist Mechelle from Our Place Boutique put together my look for the day, complete with a poufy princess dress that made me look every bit of a bridal cupcake, bangles from S. Carter, a pair of earrings I helped design, a beautiful ring my new mother-in-law gave me, and an antique diamond watch my mom and dad gave me the day of my wedding. The desserts were made courtesy of wonderfully talented women from the sex-trafficking ministry at our church, the church worship band supplied the music, and our pastor, David Chadwick, performed the ceremony.

One of the neatest parts of the day was that the wedding was a surprise. Our guests were under the impression the event was an engagement party. I've always wanted to do it that way because I've found putting the word *wedding* in a party invitation makes the event somewhat stressful and not as fun, especially for men. It was truly one of the most fun and happiest days of my life. Totally worth the long, bumpy road to get there. When the festivities were over, Tyler and I took a honeymoon break on a small island.

And in case you're wondering, we waited to have sex with each other until after we were married. Best decision ever. While we were dating, we didn't really talk about the issue for a long time, though it was a commitment both of us wanted to make. I, for one, felt that the person I was meant to marry would be the person who would be able to wait. He wouldn't groan at my decision or try to convince me otherwise. He'd totally be on board and would, along with me, put boundaries in place to help keep that commitment. Well, Tyler was that man. Waiting to have sex until after the wedding wasn't easy. Well, that's an understatement. But we knew it was something we needed to do, honoring God with our bodies and our desires. And we are so glad we did.

I can truly look back now and see how God has guided me through everything, even the hard times when I thought I'd be alone forever, and used it all to make me the person I am so that I'd be ready. As humans, we often get so focused on where we want to be in our lives, what we need to do better, things we need in order to feel complete, and worrying about our futures that we forget to stop and live in the moment. I know every girl out there with Pinterest has some variety of "Live in the Moment" quoted on one of her boards, but what does that really mean?

For so many years I have questioned why God would bring me through something like *The Bachelor* and eventually *The Bachelorette*, knowing all along I would meet my husband through church just a few miles from my house. Couldn't He have spared me all the heartbreak and humiliation? Still insecure about my past, I prayed a ton. And one day I heard God speak to me that my life now was my chance to give Him all the glory. That He had already brought me through. Goodness knows I have a long way to go to be the person He created me to be, and I'm looking forward to all God has planned not just for me but for my family.

Though marriage is wonderful in countless ways, it's not easy. Tyler and I pray together every day, we read Scripture, and we serve together. More than anything, we try to live out grace in marriage, because it gets hard sometimes. We have our share of arguments, and while I'm not proud to admit this, nine times out of ten, our fights stem from something I did, said, or felt. Of course, this is easy to see after the fact, but unfortunately not in the heat of the moment. Thing is, life has been about Ricki and me for a long time. I've grown to be very stubborn and just as independent. Which may not necessarily be bad things, but when you're married and sharing life with someone else, they can become challenges. I've had to lean on God to help me squash my pride some to see that it's okay to need Tyler or to ask for or receive help from him.

Our pastor has said that when you get married, the doors lock from the outside, meaning there's no getting out. He doesn't say this to define marriage as this oppressive or suffocating institution, but to remind those who are married to stay in the game whatever the cost. I've also heard him say that it's easy to leave your spouse, but much harder to quit on your best friend. Tyler and I take that to heart. We work hard to continue to build our friendship. To hang out and do silly things even when he comes home from work late or I'm having a rough day. We are intentional about our friendship. And I find the more we focus on that, the more connected we are.

My love life, much of which has been publicized, hasn't

been an easy road, but falling in love with God, my first love, has been a dream realized. I wonder how many of you are like the old me, trying so hard to find approval in others, especially guys, doing things for the sole purpose of getting someone to like or love you. It's a losing battle, girls. One that's sure to break your heart. There is such a comfort, a peace, found when you begin trusting God, believing that He loves you, no matter what has happened in your life, and knowing that it's enough.

If you're anything like me, you may have spent a lot of time wallowing in shame or self-pity, beating yourself up for mistakes you've made in past relationships and otherwise. Sometimes it's easy to dish out grace to others but almost impossible to show yourself the same. When you deepen your relationship with God, He helps reshape your heart and you learn, through His love, how to love yourself better. For me, this was better than any self-help book I've read.

It's easy to say you have a relationship with Him, as I did for so long, but if you're not regularly reading His Word or spending quiet time with Him in prayer, simply sharing your thoughts with Him, how can you even begin to realize your faith? The only way you can fight the negative in your life and the world is to know what you're fighting for. And the only way to do that is to practice, not just broadcast, your faith. Especially when no one's looking.

I love the way *The Message* puts Jeremiah 29:11–14: "I know what I'm doing. I have it all planned out—plans to take care of you, not abandon you, plans to give you the future you hope for. When you call on me, when you come and pray to me, I'll listen. When you come looking for me, you'll find me."

What a promise. To me, this is what matters most. While

I'm grateful for my husband, my daughter, my family, my friends, and all the opportunities I've been given, I am most taken aback by God's goodness. He woos us and invites us on an adventure headed to destinations unknown, armed with His everlasting and unfailing love. Wow! Yes, please. Definitely yes.

Acknowledgments

A.J., despite making you want to pull your hair out on multiple occasions, thank you for making this process as easy as possible. You have such a true gift, and I can't wait to see what He has in store for your future. Let's get the babies together!

Brian Hampton, Kristen Parrish, Katherine Rowley, Janene MacIvor, and the rest of the talented and creative team at Thomas Nelson who lent their talent and expertise, thanks for believing in me!

Esther, I knew the moment I met you that I wanted you on my side, and I'm so glad you were from the very beginning. Thank you for always having my back.

I couldn't write this book without thanking everyone at *The Bachelorette*. You all changed my life and taught me more about myself than I could ever imagine, good and bad! I love each of you and will count you among my true friends forever.

Specifically, Cassie, you have seen me at my best and more often at my worst and still love me despite it all. Your heart is bigger than anyone's, and I'm so lucky to count you as one of my lifelong friends. You're a tough bird for sure.

Amy, you are one of a kind and your spirit is infectious.

Thank you for always cheering me up with your awkward dances and Diet Coke in the morning. I love you!

Alycia, sometimes I think you know me better than I know myself. Thank you for always being there for me when I need you the most, whether I'm the Bachelorette or not. I love you and your sweet family so much!

Martin, thank you for being so kind to me, even when I'm "going crosses." I'm still sorry about that by the way.

Elan, what is there to say about you that hasn't been said a million times before? You're unlike anyone I've ever met in all the best ways and I love you for that.

Now on to my family,

Mom, it's hard for me to put into words how much you mean to me without crying. You've been my best friend since I was a little girl, and I just hope I can be half the mom to my children. I love you forever and like you for always.

Dad, thank you for being the first man I ever loved and showing me how I should be treated by my future husband. I love you!

Ernie, I've loved watching you grow into the amazing father and man that you are today. No one can make me laugh the way you do. I love you.

Nana and Pop Pop, we've been through so much together, and you all have become my second parents. Thank you for loving me through all the ups and downs life has taken me through. I love you both beyond words.

David Chadwick, thank you for being one of the first people to believe in me and the story He is telling through my life. Tyler and I couldn't ask for better role models than you and Marilyn. We love you both.

Ricki, we've grown up together in so many ways and yet you've taught me more about life than anyone. Being your mommy has been my greatest joy and the reason my heart smiles every day. I can't wait to see what the Lord has planned for your future because I know it's something special. I love you all the way to heaven and back.

Jennings, I prayed for you every day, and the wait was worth every minute. You've brought so much love and happiness to our house, and I fall more and more in love with you every day.

And Tyler, my best friend and truest love, where do I begin? From the moment I saw you I knew you were set apart, and I wanted you to be a part of my life forever. You have reminded me every day what God's love truly looks like by the way you love me. I love every part of who you are and can't wait to see what He has in store for our next fifty years.

About the Authors

Emily Maynard Johnson experienced the tragic and sudden loss of her fiancé, NASCAR driver Ricky Hendrick, when she was eighteen. Days after his death, she discovered she was pregnant with her now ten-year-old daughter, Ricki. Navigating life as a single mom spawned an initial whirlwind of trying to balance finding her identity as an individual and being a parent. Known best for hoping to find love on camera, Emily appeared on season 15 of *The Bachelor* and season 8 of *The Bachelorette*. In 2014, Emily found the real deal and married Tyler Johnson. A fashionista at heart, she fulfilled one lifelong dream and created her own jewelry line. Emily lives in Charlotte with her husband, Tyler; daughter, Ricki; and son, Jennings. They attend Forest Hills Church, pastored by David Chadwick.

A.J. Gregory writes about real life. She is the author of two books, *Messy Faith* and *Silent Savior*. A.J. has also partnered with amazing people on over thirty-five memoirs and self-help books, some *New York Times* bestsellers. She is known for her book collaborations with celebrities like Pattie Mallette, Justin

Bieber's mom, and Darryl Strawberry, as well as fascinating, high-profile people including a Mafia boss's wife, a Special Forces military leader, a high-class escort turned public advocate against sex trafficking, and a financially savvy blogger who averages 1.5 million readers a month. A.J. lives with her husband and their three children in the great Garden State. For more information, visit www.ajgregory.net.